Also by the author:

A Brief History of the Short-lived
Other People's Lives
Unfamiliar Weather

Jonas in Frames

an epic

Chris Hutchinson
Goose Lane Editions | icehouse poetry

Copyright © 2014 by Chris Hutchinson.

All rights reserved. No part of this work may be reproduced or used in any form or by any means, electronic or mechanical, including photocopying, recording or any retrieval system, without the prior written permission of the publisher or a licence from the Canadian Copyright Licensing Agency (Access Copyright). To contact Access Copyright, visit www.accesscopyright.ca or call 1-800-893-5777.

Edited by Evie Christie.
Cover and page design by Chris Tompkins.
On the front cover: "Business Superman" photo detail bizior photography, www.bizior.com; "Urban Teenager" photo detail www.istockphoto.com; "Inquisitive" photo detail www.sxc.hu; "Grungy Paper" www.deviantart.com.
On the back cover: "Banana" photo www.sxc.hu.
Printed in Canada.
10 9 8 7 6 5 4 3 2 1

Library and Archives Canada Cataloguing in Publication

Hutchinson, Chris, 1972-, author
  Jonas in frames : an epic / Chris Hutchinson.

Novel in poetic form.
Issued in print and electronic formats.
ISBN 978-0-86492-435-3 (pbk.). — ISBN 978-0-86492-579-4 (epub)

  I. Title.

PS8615.U823J65 2014   C813'.6   C2013-907306-X
                                      C2013-907307-8

Goose Lane Editions acknowledges the generous support of the Canada Council for the Arts, the Government of Canada through the Canada Book Fund (CBF), and the Government of New Brunswick through the Department of Tourism, Heritage and Culture.

Goose Lane Editions
500 Beaverbrook Court, Suite 330
Fredericton, New Brunswick
CANADA E3B 5X4
www.gooselane.com

Of all plots and actions the episodic are the worst.
— Aristotle

*Ah! is there one who ever has been young,
Nor needs a monitory voice to tame
The pride of virtue, and of intellect?
And is there one, the wisest and the best
Of all mankind, who does not sometimes wish
For things which cannot be, who would not give,
If so he might, to duty and to truth
The eagerness of infantine desire?*
— William Wordsworth

The bottom of the sea is cruel.
— Hart Crane

CONTENTS

Prologue   *9*

ONE

Shivers and Shakes	*15*
Lab Notes	*17*
Jonas in Paroxysms	*18*
The Psychiatrist's Office	*22*
Lab Notes	*27*
Jail	*28*
Bananas	*32*
Lab Notes	*37*
The Desert	*38*
Mercer	*42*
Scar	*48*
Lab Notes	*51*
The Pigeon	*52*

TWO

New York	*55*
Frank's Place	*61*
Lab Notes	*67*
Relationship	*68*
Lab Notes	*77*
Too Far North	*78*
Lab Notes	*85*
One Year Drifting Backwards and Forwards through Time	*86*
Factotum	*93*
Lab Notes	*98*

Back in the City of Broken Glass	99
Lab Notes	106
Gymnastics	107

THREE

Mr. Sock	113
Self-Diagnosis	118
In the Freezing Rain	123
Lab Notes	126
All You Get	127
More Bad News	129
Lab Notes	135
Cab Ride	136
Forgetting	140
The Good Life	144
Lab Notes	147
Jonas in Frames	148
Fuck It	150
The Ferry to the Kingdom of the Afterlife	152
Lab Notes	156
Back on Land	157
These Happy Carefree Days	159
Smack	163
Village Life Nostalgia	174
Lab Notes	180
Notes for a Poem (Revised as a Flashback)	181
The Heron	183
Lab Notes: Addendum	186
Epilogue	187
Acknowledgements	190

Prologue

It is not an extraordinary existence at the corner of West Twelfth Street and Nowhere. How can he justify the air moving through his lungs, the blood through his heart, the sweat through his pores?

Jonas lives in a small ground-level apartment, which wicks the summer's late afternoon sun through the living room window. Dusky heat spills over a frayed floral brocade sofa and floods across the length of the unvarnished hardwood floor.

A Leo, twenty-nine as of today, he is average looking and of medium build — though he sometimes worries that his head is too big for his body, and dreams of one day owning a blue felt fedora that actually fits. He's got a real melon, a planetoid, a brain with a veritable mind of its own, and an imagination that won't quit. His sofa, he sees, is fizzing with dust motes — punctuation marks of his life's invisible script!

To beat the heat and to celebrate the evening, Jonas drinks Chinese cooking wine with ice at his kitchen's bar counter. He wishes Helen of Troy were here, or Cleopatra, or a young Jane Fonda. He wishes he wouldn't wish so much, or at least wish for practical things like stocks or government bonds. But money is the obsession of people other than himself — the word *career*, an echo from a faraway universe, from a time before the cursèd deluge known as the Devil's Water.

He peels the label away from the bottle, revealing a window of dark glass.

Bananas, he read somewhere, contain a natural antidepressant, their soft flesh a materialized form of sunlight. So he tries to remember to mash half of one into his Corn Flakes each morning, but too often he forgets. His freezer, subsequently, has become a morgue for black bananas he can't bring himself to discard.

So so so... cracking another ice cube into his glass, he fills the tray's vacant squares with water then tops up his wine. He's not sad, just resigned to his solitude and poverty, and the steady purr of traffic along Twelfth Street lulls him into a feeling of detached security as night comes on...

A siren cuts the air, warping into the far distance to indicate yet another otherworldly emergency. Someone's chamomile tea-drinking aunt must have fallen asleep while crocheting, and her menthol cigarette, dropping from her ashtray into a cardboard box full of newly made doilies, must have set the whole house ablaze.

Or someone's cousin must have gone off his meds and wandered into traffic thinking the oncoming headlights were the welcoming eyes of ethereal beings.

Or someone's ex-husband's lone journey through time must have ended with manuscript pages ripped into shreds and tossed like so many suicide notes over the guardrail of the Lions Gate Bridge.

Jonas thinks: *Disasters surround me! Seas of confusion!* He refills his glass, sets sail to swelling breakers — but forgets to tie himself to the mast...

The moon comes up full and squints through the branches and heart-shaped leaves of the chestnut. Now is the hour when silence unfolds its want ad for remembrance, when Jonas must resist punishing himself for everything he's either never attempted, or tried and failed at.

His father used to shout at him, "name *one* thing you can do, *one* thing that's useful, *one* thing you're good at!" Then his teachers joined in, his gurus, his guides, and his friends.

The Voice in his head wants to speak, taunting him with the line: *In the Kingdom of the Afterlife, nothing's ironic* — which he thinks to write down, but doesn't. Not yet.

Instead he swims out to his sofa, now floating in moonlight, where the dust motes have turned to vibrating stars. Draining his glass, then stretching out and closing his eyes, he begins: *It is not an extraordinary existence at the corner of West Twelfth Street and Nowhere...*

[*Here several pages have been lost.*]

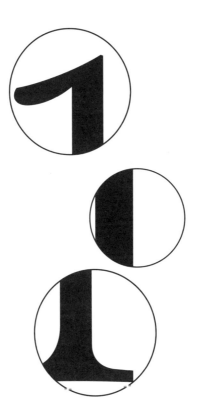

Shivers and Shakes

Jonas, what is happening to you? What is this hammering in the blood, this bullet ricocheting through your brain, this force that seizes and shakes you by the limbs? Your thoughts are all Celtic knots, and your stomach quakes. Perhaps it was something poisonous you drank?

It's as if you are freezing, these tremors rippling through your flesh wanting to beat warmth back into your blood. And your skin *is* cold — the surface of your body feels like the surface of a mirror — while your insides burn and roil.

It started like this: you were dozing in half sleep, in the spotlight of your mind, and haunted by the astringent scent of silver polish which seemed to be emanating from your own breath. At the window two moths fluttering around the moon's reflected light were casting crazy shadows across the wall above the foot of your bed, and as you watched them morph into trembling hands you felt a bolus of sorrow welling up behind your solar plexus, then moving through your esophagus and into your throat.

The prospect of tears panicked you — it had been years since you wept — until you heard the disembodied counsel of that well-meaning presence, not the Voice, but a feminine whisper soothing with assurances: *go ahead, laisse-toi aller, you'll feel better soon, voilà un gentil garçon, tiens, tiens, mon amour, there you are*... You hadn't thought to argue with or resist this incorporeal self, though maybe you should have. Maybe if you hadn't relinquished your strength, if you hadn't floated in that brief moment of acquiescence, then those first stumbling sobs wouldn't have pitched you into this full-throttled seizure.

Your crying feels like dying. A pitiless power attends the storms of electrons embodied in the mystery of your nerves. O Heavenly Muse, what fun! Maybe you have epilepsy, or cerebral palsy? Is this how your story ends, having never begun? You are under attack from invisible enemies. Something has short-circuited, the movie of your life all jitter, stutter, and skip. Ganglions gone gaga, you shudder, twitch, blink hot tears. Enslaved to Saint Vitus. Body in revolt. Teeth clenched. Paroxysms…

Lab Notes

Our subject in question, Subject X, though volatile and often in flux, has yet to transgress the parameters we have set. In fact, Subject X's squirming and surging and struggling against our boundaries, as well as his secret wish for a "FTW" bicep tattoo, only serves to reinforce said boundaries (engineered to approximate muscle tissue, to grow stronger through the resistance of force) and to weaken the subject's own strength over time. This is a positive result. As expected, the more virulent the mutation, the more rigidly it is contained.

Jonas in Paroxysms

On Vancouver Island, in grade three, Jonas marries his rosy-cheeked sweetheart, Gretchen Snyder, between the rows of bike racks beside the Big Hill. This is Friday, after school. (Yes, Jonas, sometimes life is grand!)

He rides home at top speed, the peeling paint on his BMX bike's rusty handlebars vibrating in the wind. Perhaps he even feels the hair follicles on his arms twitching in the rush of air, fluttering through every golden superlative.

On Monday, at morning recess, Jonas discovers Gretchen pushing Scott Gamble up against the Kissing Wall behind the gym. Life is over then. Something breaks and slips loose like a chain off a bike on a downhill ride. Jonas loses focus, swerves, and falls through a Jonas-shaped hole in the world…

There is the acrid taste of failure, a confusion of depth, the jewelled eyes of minnows, the caressing seaweed strands where breakers wing to shore, and the sun above, a phosphorescent lure.

Next, the Blue Heron is the neck tattoo of choice of the clownish art-school dropouts whose figures sift the air made soft as flakes of gold in the last rays of sun on Saint-Laurent Boulevard. They are trying to ignore a furrow-browed man who shakes coins inside his cup. It is the remnants of himself that he is rattling, of a life answerable to no one.

Later — in a piano bar in a parallel universe, on the ledge of a window with a view of the muddy Yukon River glinting through a screen of birch — wildflowers wilt inside a ceramic vase. Heads hang abjectly. Purple petals squeezed shut in perpetual sleep. Exhausted hands of leaves, crumpled, submissive to the pull of earth. Beside the window, suspended by two chains, a framed plaque reads:

> I wanted the gold, and I sought it;
> I scrabbled and mucked like a slave.
> Was it famine or scurvy — I fought it;
> I hurled my youth into a grave.

But no, this is skid row, the Downtown Eastside, a room with a view of Chinatown, and the beginning of everything Jonas will never comprehend, a riddle he solves by simply dissolving — muscles shifting, loosening, strength leaking out through punctured flesh and streaming into the neon lights reflected on wet streets.

Meanwhile, Jonas sleeps several metres beneath the sea, inside a leafing live oak, where he skims through volume six of an old *Encyclopaedia Britannica*. Even in this place, how the past continues to dictate his dreams, telling his story, which, Jonas reads, is reflected in the constellations wheeling round Polaris.

Then, whey-faced and wry-sensed, he is lost in the crush of pedestrian traffic. Wafts of air, metallic, putrid, blend with his body's sweat. Each pore breathes out a little filth, breathes in the streets of Brooklyn. With every step he becomes more convinced that his evil twin is a bridegroom soaking in a bath of ice-cold Perrier.

Or, prone to speculations about visitors from space, to paranoid conjectures about being scrutinized and dissected, to suspicions that he has been programmed by nefarious algorithms, and to the habit of drifting off into any number of subjective universes — perhaps Jonas writes words inside his head to resist being *himself* written on, or through.

Now sea air swells the wooden doors shut. Inside a story set in the Land of Fog, stuck in a warehouse wallpapered with cancan girls dancing in endless rows — a flashy decorating idea from some bygone era — Jonas touches his index finger to his nose, confirming that yes, in a previous life he drove an unlicensed cab in São Paulo. Then in 1971 he is born on the doorstep of Mount Royal, a not-so-empty vessel.

But by 1974, although his father's mind has turned to fractals and his mother's soul has flown the wrong way through time to relive her sins in the Centre-du-Québec, they somehow all manage to move out west. Backdropped by blue mountains, cedar sentinels guard the sea's edge. Jonas recalls the fern pollen, which looked like rust as it stuck to the white vinyl siding of his father's garage, as the image of the beginning of a lifelong depression.

And it is here, out west, while attending Clearview Elementary School, where Jonas marries for the first and last time, then fights in the Great Pinecone War for the Big

Hill — here, where the girls wear pigtails and Daisy Duke overalls and the boys in their gumboots are indistinguishable from the grief-stricken fishermen of Nanoose Bay.

His teacher's voice has followed him through the years: *If you're too lazy to learn your multiplication tables then you won't be able to move up a grade, and later in life when you don't have a job, what will you do and where will you go when you don't have any money?*

After Gretchen and the War, there is Cecily, then Melanie. Then comes grade four.

The Psychiatrist's Office

What the fuck. Jonas needs help, a steadier point of reference, or some happy pills. But for now, trapped in this waiting room, his mission is to appear spiritually composed, and to avoid eye contact with the silver-sideburned, top-hatted man sitting across from him, who keeps shivering his brow above a battered issue of *Elle*. Straining his legs into a painful lotus, Jonas closes his eyes and attempts to focus on why he is here...

He is used to certain malfunctions, like the not-being-able-to-get-out-of-bed. He has become resigned to the broken switch in his head. (It is no secret that there is a sequence of switches which, when triggered, causes a functioning body to activate — if only to shuffle to the computer to check an email account or a weather report or a fetish-porn site. In a healthy subject this initial action will lead to the triggering of other switches, and how quickly and efficiently this exemplar of normalcy — charmed with élan, vitality, chi — will flow towards the next purposeful activity, like poetry editing or shoe weatherproofing or furious masturbation, etc.)

Yes, Jonas has lived with himself long enough to know that he is somehow different, and that there is no escaping. He knows there is an imperceptible impetus, which most take for granted until that morning it just isn't there — that morning when, despite the mind's ability to conceive of several well-founded reasons to rise from the bed, the body remains inert, heavy, and suddenly the pernicious thought occurs that to move, in the grand scheme of things, will really make no difference at all.

Jonas knows there is in every feeling thing a governing impulse toward movement — that which jolts life along from point A to point B — and that to be *human* is to be driven by the need, if not to get up and go, then at least to be worried by the urge to squirm or to fidget. Only the sick are idle, lame, impotent. (Only the *inhuman*, like you, Jonas.)

At other times his lethargy is supplanted by an anxiety bright and angular as shards of glass. The thought of the difference of scale between his domestic habitat — with its small comforts and possessions — and the ramshackle expanse of the external universe — with its psych wards and opera houses, its prison systems and income tax forms, its peacock feathers and smelling salts, its drone attacks and insights into lucid dreaming research grants — is enough to send shivers of vertigo from his toes up his spine and back down again, jarring loose two irreconcilable needs: to hide and to break free.

All of this is familiar — the yo-yoing between depressive and manic states. It has all happened before — usually in winter when the rain drapes its chain-link fence around each lit window and streetlight, making strange everything which once seemed safe or promising.

But he has never lost control of his legs and arms like that. He has never, before last night, gone into an hour-long spasm —

Opening his eyes, Jonas discovers the creepy top-hatted man has been replaced by a white rabbit in a pink sundress who is directing Jonas with her nose towards the glow of a half-open door at the end of a dimly lit corridor...

In the doctor's office, he is asked questions: Does he hear voices? Is Jonas his given name? Any shortness of breath? Who is his emergency contact? What year is it? Was the footage of the moon landing faked?

The doctor is a sallow-complexioned raver with silver-sequined slippers and a shaved head. They sit across from one another, a battered steel desk cluttered with disposable coffee cups and stacks of dishevelled papers between them. "Call me Oliver," he says. Oliver's eyes are green capsules, he wears fashionable glasses with rims and arms as clear as the lenses, and he has a habit of either clearing his throat or saying the word "wow" after each of his odd questions.

Call me Ishmael, says Jonas to himself.

On the wall just above Oliver's shiny cranium Jonas spots what at first appears to be some sort of psychedelic pop art from the seventies. But no, it is a matted textbook illustration showing a stickman whose aura is exploding in a rainbow of concentric arcs, starting with a small white halo around the head labelled "EGO" and radiating outwards to the far edges of the diagram where the dark blue realm of the "COLLECTIVE UNCONSCIOUS" threatens to expand beyond the frame.

Sitting up in his seat, Jonas adjusts his sightline so that the colours appear to emanate from Oliver's skull. Suddenly, everything makes sense.

Jonas, which is not his *only* name (we want you to believe that your real name is Jonas Ignatius Hallgrimsson the Third), wants to tell Oliver, who is now exactly what he *appears* to be (a fleshy marionette), that Dizzy's trumpet sounds just like the brass it was made of. Jonas wants to describe why no one blows kisses anymore without an appointment, and how any clairvoyant worth knowing should know that any trip to the Pyrenees will be an unholy disaster.

Oliver blinks through his space-age specs, swallows in slow motion, then coughs distractedly while Jonas is left to wonder if the face he sees in the mirror, a visage he sometimes mistakes as his father's back from the grave, will one day start to talk on its own. He thinks and he thinks: *When the Winnebago comes into my life, will I take it as a giant microwave dinner, hot from the oven? Will my nipples pucker up for a kiss? O Manhattan was merely the voodoo charm I kept in my front pocket even as I weighed the anchor of my homesickness. Now I wear a raincloud for a hat. Now I douse my temples with a cologne made from the crushed memory glands of the filthy rich...*

In some other room, the questions and throat clearings and wows continue: "Heart palpitations?" *Ahem.* "Thoughts of suicide?" *Ahem.* "Spontaneous dancing?" *Wow.* "Bananas? Drugs? Scars? Pets?" *Wow. Wow. Wow.*

From some other world, someone is asking: "Earworms? Nostalgia? Artistic ambitions?"

All of this is familiar. It has all happened before. The white rabbit and the top-hatted man are in cahoots. The evil stickman is communicating telepathically through Oliver, though it's obvious to Jonas that Oliver is innocent.

Lab Notes

Our mechanisms must remain invisible in the form of well-established tropes, or appear disguised as the opposite of their true raisons d'être. The power to choose freely, for example, is represented by binary pairs that are, in actuality, cooperative functions of a singular Law. Thus, as long as Conservatives with PCs drink Coke and Liberals with MacBooks drink Pepsi, equilibrium will be maintained and power remain in the hands of the Overseers.

Jail

In the drunk tank, Jonas recalls having read that the interaction between certain medications and alcohol can lead to a significant increase in one's risk of illness, injury, loneliness, temporal displacement, or even death.

His t-shirt pulled over his eyes to shield them from the buzzing electric lights mounted in mesh cages on every wall, Jonas is a fetus crumpled in the corner. His resting spot smells of rotten lemons in a rusted tin.

Jolted by the sound of rushing water, Jonas peers through the thin fabric of his shirt and spies what appears to be a barrel-shaped gnome? Elf? Leprechaun? No, he surmises that the creature perched atop the metal toilet in the opposite corner is actually a dwarf. "Hin-sane hin the membrane! I'm hin-sane, I got no brain!" raps the dwarf while flushing the toilet in cadenced accompaniment. One of the dwarf's eyes is a vortex of black leather, while the other is a laser shooting its beam right through Jonas's last chance to fall back asleep.

After several more flushes the small figure jumps down, pulls up his little jeans and, with a slow limping gait, saunters over to Jonas's side of the cell. Emerging from his shirt-cave, Jonas peers up at a hovering face, all pale and nebulous except for the black patch. Trying to look only at the dwarf's good side, Jonas manages a weak, "Can I help you?"

"I'm-a buss you *hup*!" barks the dwarf in a voice that sounds like a clown horn. "Stand *hup*!"

"Why? What for?" says Jonas, not sure how to react.

"I'm-a *smash* you if you don't get *hup*! I need a *fight*!"

Jonas thinks, considers, weighs his response, then misspeaks, "Yo mister, uh, dude man, maybe we could join forces, maybe plot an escape? You know what Nelson Mandela said? Freedom's just another word for nothing left to lose! Or, anyway...*something* like that."

Menacing one fist, the dwarf seems about to swing an invisible hatchet down into Jonas's forehead. "I can't be locked *hup* with hanyone, *dude maaaan*. I'll go *hinsane*! I need my hown *cell*. I need to be *alone*! Guess what I do for a living? I work at a *bank*! I got a *yacht* and I drive a fuckin' Mercedes-*Benz*! Stand hup, or I'll pound yer *skull in*!"

These last two syllables go on and on, not recurring in the dwarf's mouth, which is twisted up in a knot, but echoing from somewhere far away in time and space, *skull in skull in skull in*...

The eye patch is an evil moon. It is an eye patch-shaped hole in the universe.

Liberty, equality, fraternity, thinks Jonas, *anyway, fuck that.*

Rising stiffly to his knees, Jonas seizes the child-sized man, stuffing the surprisingly ample head under one armpit and squeezing. The more Jonas levers and stretches the squirming dwarf's neck, the faster his little arms flap in ridiculous haymakers, fists bumping weakly against Jonas's shoulders and back. His burst of impotent fury exhausted, the dwarf begins to stamp one foot while making phlegmy rattle sounds inside his nose. With his free hand Jonas reaches in to claw at the dwarf's eye patch, somehow managing to rip the patch away from the dwarf's skull while simultaneously tossing the limp body to the cement floor like the peel of a banana — then Jonas has to catch himself, to wrench himself into the present, to focus on the diminutive size of his opponent and, adjusting for fairness relative to volume, density, and height, to stop himself from jumping to his feet and kicking the sprawling dwarf repeatedly in his teeth —

Two guards rush in. One has the devilish snout of a fruit bat. Suddenly it's summer, years into the future, and everything's the colour of a ripe peach. Then it's too late. New York Harbor turns blue. The subway is a steel wind playing havoc's xylophone —

Once the guards and the dwarf have disappeared inside a series of choked screams and the harsh thunder of metal cleaving itself, Jonas adjusts his new patch over one eye, stretching the strap to a tight fit. Cupping his other eye with his palm, he falls into a snowstorm where a pigeon appears on a fire escape rung doing a robot dance with its head and neck. *There can be no alliances*, says the bird with its apple-seed stare.

The lights in their cages are still buzzing. Half awake, dreaming through the bars of his fingers, Jonas sees the bilious rays spreading down the walls and over the cement floor to pick out stray pubic hairs, flecks of old and new blood, and brown bits and pieces of who knows what.

But soon Jonas is walking the Styrofoam corridors towards a seascape made of melting green capsules. The sky is a bulletproof Plexiglas bank teller window with a black speaking hole.

Hello? Anyone? But the bank must be closed.

(Tomorrow, we'll make sure you forget most of this — except for the dwarf's revealed eye socket, which will linger.)

Bananas

The day he comes home, he loses his sense of identity, his sense of direction — living in a one-room apartment in this falling down, three-storey dump encroached on by a tangle of overgrown holly. The smells are of the old and forgotten: unseen mouse nests beneath the water-damaged hardwood, oxidized copper, mildew, and rotting plaster. The eyesore of the block, with its peeling paint and faltering frame, the house is a poetic anachronism, an indelible remnant of pre-gentrification.

He has been here too long. His freezer is jammed with dead bananas and there are as many drained beer cans amassed under the kitchen sink. He wants to leave the whole mess behind, to start over, maybe reinvent his story as a picaresque!

But first he wanders his own neighbourhood, thinking of himself as Odysseus disguised as a beggar, and marvelling at the cornices and columns of his neighbours' Craftsman-style homes — all recently renovated and brightly trimmed. What, exactly, is he doing here? There are cats perched on porch banisters like little rajahs. There are wind chimes made of seashells and sea glass hanging from the eaves of gabled roofs. There are yards with old iron washtubs repurposed as herb gardens, and rusted bicycles ready to serve as latticeworks for the summer's tomatoes. There are boys on trampolines, girls in tire swings and fathers and mothers in lawn chairs unfolded beneath banana daiquiri skies!

Fuck poetry, he thinks. He could use a cigarette, and a life partner, someone who will spank his ass, and make better decisions. He needs a mousetrap, lemon-scented dish soap, and an important-sounding job, something to show off at his upcoming high school reunion (which you will attend, via the satellite link we have provided, inside your head).

It is the beginning of spring in the Pacific Northwest, yet despite the lengthening days, his unhappiness lingers. It tingles and aches. Never mind the budding magnolias' little pink fists, or the echoing laughter of daffodils. The rain has started again, and he feels like shit. He feels like *Krapp's Last Tape* permanently held over.

His depression is seasonal. If this is the early fall of his life, then how long until he plunges into a major middle-aged bummer?

The eye patch is forcing him to swing his head around to see things and its strap is chafing his ear, so he rips the one-winged bat from his face and tosses it onto the roof of an old grey Volvo. A threshold opens suddenly on his left where the sun appears, peeking out from the clouds and taking the form of a bumblebee perched on the carved tip of a mammoth tusk. The medication isn't working. His mind is all *National Geographic*, pages flipping between scenes of emperor penguins marching through ice troughs and images of naked children scrounging through mountains of garbage in search of edible scraps.

Each step causes his knees to vibrate slightly, as if troubled by a mild electrical current. *Perhaps I should start dating*, thinks Jonas, *stop drifting... maybe even stop drinking, this time for good.* He wants his forest back, his childhood image of forgetting. He needs an oiled-up shoulder rub, a washbasin full of raffle tickets, and to know that to have written that book Dostoevsky must have actually killed someone—

Jonas wonders if someone is following him, photographing his habits and behaviours, documenting his movements, maybe even recording his thoughts? The grey Volvo chugs past, ferrying the eye patch along towards its next adventure. The car's great grey cloud of exhaust suspiciously obscures the driver's identity...

Before entering the dépanneur at the corner of Sherbrooke and Saint-Denis, Jonas realizes that he has walked a very long way, that he has crossed several provinces and time zones, that he is hungry, and that he has no money, and will probably have no money for some time. (In fact, you will soon get lost trying to negotiate the various banana breads, banana pancakes, and banana cream pies the buffet of first-world poverty offers its discerning clientele. For you, whose social mobility tends to slide in the wrong direction—though perhaps not to the very bottom, as we've given you the names and numbers of several mental health care workers and food bank volunteers — for you, your survival will depend on your ability to survey the field, to evaluate the stakes associated with the various positions thereon, and to obtain a prescription for more oblong yellow happy pills.)

Jonas sidles furtively up to the counter where the clerk, a dumpy kid in a t-shirt that says "VIVE LE QUÉBEC LIBRE!" skateboards back and forth, pivoting to the beat of hard techno pounding from an old ghetto blaster mounted on the wall beside the cigarette cases. "Hey, boss, quelle heure est-il?" Jonas inquires. But the kid doesn't respond, so Jonas goes on, "Did you know that thanks to the Higgs boson in about ten billion years the whole universe is going to implode at light speed?" and just as the kid is leaning his shoulders into his next wheelie-turn, Jonas grabs a banana from off the counter and stuffs it down the front of his pants. "Good Christ, I guess I should get back to my own country before the language police come!" he barks, startling the kid who fails in his pivot, skids, and drops behind the counter with a sodden thud.

Meanwhile, Jonas has bolted out the door to find himself magically transported back inside a west coast drizzle which immediately chills his wrists and the back of his neck…

He is sick of this sham spring, this malingering season, and these gaps of missing time. Soon more rain will come — all the seconds in a day turning to splashing notes, clear arteries pulsing down every windowpane — and it will saturate the roots of the holly trees and turn the ripening earth to black mud.

Soon his whole house, with its mouldering odours and untold histories, will be sucked into a Charybdis-like sinkhole.

Time to leave town again, this time forever, Jonas thinks, throwing the yellow peel dramatically into the pale sky behind him, *or live here, between Nothing and Nowhere, and learn to survive on rainwater, bananas, and air.*

Back home, Jonas discovers months' worth of junk mail and final notices in the hall, and that — precisely because he had hoped it wouldn't — the power has been shut off. He dares not open the fridge or the freezer. Ignoring his appetite, lying down on the decomposing hardwood in the accumulating dusk, his arms crossed over his chest, Jonas listens to the silvery squeals from the street below from the children he imagines are chasing each other in endless circles, in irrefutable delight, over wet sidewalks smudged with apple blossoms.

Somewhere the banana peel waits for a careless foot. Somewhere the eye patch bears blind witness. The more the night comes on, the farther away he hopes to go...

Lab Notes

Further observations and tests must be conducted as a few irregularities have appeared on neural scans, and glitches in behaviour, though expected, are not always within the range predicted by our market efficiency models. Also, in order to determine whether Subject X's Atari video game nostalgia is the result of an error in our methodology, we must first divine the impact of long-term-return fashion anomalies, such as wearing deck shoes with pants rolled halfway up the shins.

The Desert

"This history of *Arabian Nights*," explains Jonas in a rush, "is complicated, just like the evolution of the sandpiper's pencil-like bill, or the story of how amyl nitrite transformed a whole generation of c-c-c-club c-c-c-*culture*." But it would seem that Oliver doesn't care enough to listen. It would seem that to Oliver everything and everyone in the world can be divided into one of two categories, circular or square, and that the squares, like Jonas, are always bringing Oliver down.

And even though it is Friday, and even though Jonas is on a manic upswing, and even though Oliver is wearing fancy light-adapting photochromic glasses, his favourite bunny rabbit t-shirt, and brand-new lime-green Converse Kicks — downtown Phoenix is dead.

They amble across thoroughfares lined with spindly palm trees whose perfectly spherical tops appear to have been manicured by militant cheerleaders. *Dr. Seuss would never live here*, notes Jonas to his increasingly benighted and ever-withering inner self. And son of a bitch! — how did he ever think it was a good idea to befriend and wander around America stoned with his psychiatrist?

"Seasonal affective disorder" is what Oliver had discovered inside Jonas's head, subsequently recommending a rainbow of prescriptions plus a quick getaway to the Valley of the Sun, where some of Oliver's oldest and shadiest friends were apparently hiding out, afraid of some nameless retribution from above.

The address they are looking for but will never find — a spot teeming, according to Oliver, with YouTube celebrities, New Age healers, and grant proposal writing experts — is a large hotel which apparently looks like a birthday cake, but without icing or candles. Paris Hilton, according to local lore, once dry-heaved herself into a coma in a corner of the lobby behind a large potted aloe.

"Someone must have dropped a neutron bomb," Jonas says. "It's as if everything living has been vaporized, but the infrastructure is still intact."

"Not true. Wow, look, there's Samuel Beckett," says Oliver, tapping one rubberized toe at a grey wad of chewing gum squashed into the sidewalk. "See his crinkly forehead?"

"More like Hemingway in an oversized turtleneck."

"I feel like a pill bug pioneering across someone's newly cemented garage floor," says Oliver.

"I feel like Jesus in the desert, but with nothing to tempt me," says Jonas.

"It's a dry sauna, this heat."

"It's a white-hot tundra."

"Look, the sky's changing colour. Is this the blue screen of death I see before me?"

"No, it's a Mark Rothko."

The two walk side by side into the gathering shadows of twilight, arms and legs swinging languidly in sync. They are, and they are not, the best of friends. (Jonas, why do you so often feel like this, both disappointed and hopeful? Why are you such a sucker for bad bets, scorpion candies on a stick, and adventures in ambivalence?)

After lighting a cigarette and theatrically whooshing a mouthful of smoke up towards a newly risen sliver of moon, Jonas starts jogging backwards in front of Oliver. "Hey, doc, how is it you can make the decision to stop breathing, at least for a minute, but you can't think hard enough to slow your own heart, or put your liver on pause, or tell your spleen to go for a smoke break?"

"The brain, you *blockhead*," says Oliver, rapping a knuckle against his glistening bald scalp.

"The skull is the brain's woooomb!" Jonas intones.

Oliver continues: "The brain is an organ you can easily turn off. It's a matter of will — of the *will* to will. And speaking of *blockheads*, did I ever tell you," he says, pausing to flip a small blue pill into his mouth and swallowing it down with a quick shake of his head. "Wow, did I ever tell you how my goddamn stepmother once had the *nerve* to sneak onto the set of *Hollywood Squares*?" He goes on, lost now, yet content to coast fecklessly forever along the desert's vapid passageways. "Or how my friends used to call me *the bingo-kid*, or how I once touched MC Hammer's knee and called him *Mr. Square Pants*, even after he told me I *couldn't?*"

But Jonas has stopped jogging and he stares up at the sliver of moon, which has miraculously dilated to become a disk sparkling like tinfoil in a microwave. Oliver, who likes to pretend he can see perfectly at night through his fantastic lenses, moves on ahead, mumbling, "You know those eighties rap stars come to Arizona now for cheap plastic surgery, and they all vote *Republican?*"

Jonas replies, but to himself alone: *I'm not superficial, just cool in a way to suggest that beneath my glossy surface exists a deep and profound source of suffering.*

The disk in the sky is expanding. A brightening globe, it pulses and continues to grow, until its hem touches and spills over the earth, a light that liquefies and enraptures—

Later, no matter how hard they try, neither Oliver nor Jonas can talk about what happens next.

Mercer

Far from home, Jonas is clambering over a frozen moraine — possibly the remnant of some long-ago Titan's wall — when he spies what looks like a stand of futuristic totem poles. But drawing closer, he finds himself staring up at three towering radio masts.

In the hollow beneath one of the towers he builds a torso-shaped pagoda, not from stones but from all the beer cans he finds and flattens with his boot heel. "Tell me," he asks his friend who isn't there, "what's the use trying to reach you now? Let's say the score is one to zero, but I don't know who's ahead, or who's been left behind."

The beer-can pagoda winks. Jonas shivers. Wind drones through the steel lattices. There is always a crow travelling the thin beam of a sundog, skating above the black horizon away from the light.

This scene is cast from a memory of events that never occurred. Even so, it is the place Jonas often comes to, just as he's falling asleep, where he talks with Mercer's disembodied presence.

Mercer, with his politician smile and herringbone bowties, was not someone Jonas ever planned to trust. Over a decade ago they had attended the same high school, but while Jonas had consorted with the few other oddballs like himself — mostly geeks and slackers — Mercer had kept company with a socialite set who all seemed destined for the kind of neon-bright future the eighties engendered in the hopes of spoiled adolescents.

It isn't until Jonas lands in the emergency room one night — after having been bashed by an unexpectedly flung-out car door and toppled from his bicycle — that he and Mercer actually look into one another's eyes and speak.

Jonas is hobbling out from a surgery room, one pant leg soiled with blood, his stitched-up thigh stiff and stinging, when he spots Mercer in the waiting area bent over in his seat. At first he thinks Mercer is suffering from abdominal pain then sees he is only talking intently into a cellphone.

After flipping his phone shut, Mercer looks up and puts on his grin. They shake hands, exchange bits of information, awkwardly at first. Apparently Mercer's six-year-old daughter has come down with chicken pox. "Oh, it looks like she'll be just fine," says Mercer, cheerily. "But try explaining to the ex-wife," he adds, gesturing to the phone in his blazer pocket, "that this isn't some Greek tragedy in the *making*."

Jonas is amazed at Mercer's attire, his bowtie matched to a dark grey suit complete with a waistcoat and watch chain, and offset by a green-with-white-polka-dots silken pocket square where the polka dots are actually tiny skulls. Where Mercer's daughter is, and why — if everything's fine — Mercer is still waiting here, remains a mystery. Then Mercer says, "So tell me something more about *you*," and with these words, his aspect changes. He straightens his shoulders, frowns slightly, as if on the verge of a grave theme, and leans in. This is not the Mercer Jonas remembers. Here is the visage of solicitude, dark eyes the still waters of a reflecting pool.

Slightly taken aback, and not sure where to begin, Jonas relates the evening's events, describing his recent bike wreck. He sketches the panicked car owner speeding him to the hospital, squealing her tires around corners while pleading with him not to sue since not only had her insurance expired, but her licence had just been revoked.

Then Jonas finds himself telling a story about Mary, poor Mary, the sprite-sized girl with buggy eyes he had met recently in an Anna Karenina chat room and who, two nights ago in the real world, had tried to jump from a sixth floor window...

They are out drinking at a dance club, celebrating the windfall of cash Mary has received from her recently deceased cross-dressing uncle, Lucille. But over the course of the night, as the house music transitions to the darker side of dubstep, so Mary's mood shifts from wildly outgoing to introspective and vicious. Her saucer eyes narrow to slots. Sure, they happily neck and fondle one another on top of a picnic table in the park on their way home — but once they enter Jonas's apartment lobby, Mary, suddenly shaking her head and flailing her arms at some invisible swarm of flying insects, shrieks, "This money is a *curse*!" Scrunching her face into a grotesque mask and talking in a voice gone suddenly hoarse, she goes on to claim that she is possessed by a demon and wants to die. Then she bolts for the staircase.

"Maybe it was a bad mix of booze and Wellbutrin. Who knows?" says Jonas to Mercer, and continues…

More bewildered than concerned, Jonas gives Mary a half-hearted chase upstairs. Her squirming torso is floating high above the sidewalk — the exposed small of her back pale in the moonlight, her arms stretched out in a superhero pose as she tosses crumpled bills towards the pedestrians below — before Jonas can grab her feet and haul her inside. They struggle. She kicks him in the groin, spits in his face then, whirling around, smashes the window's glass with the side of one fist. Her wrist gashed open, blood spatters the hallway floor. Backing away, Jonas watches as she begins painting a horror-show smiley face with the tip of one shoe, adding dollar signs for eyes. Laughing at first, then grunting, almost choking, she finally sinks into a stunned silence. Her eyelids are closed but fluttering as her head falls towards her chest just as her knees begin to give, so Jonas lunges, lifting her suddenly limp body over his shoulder — which is when the dreadlocked hippie appears, like a ghost out of thin air, inquiring timidly if everything's cool.

"I tell him everything's good," says Jonas, "I say I've got the situation in hand and everything's golden." He chuckles as he finishes the story. "Broken glass and blood everywhere, I've got a comatose girl fireman-style over my shoulder, and this wannabe Rasta just smiles and vanishes back inside his apartment."

Mercer doesn't laugh, seeming detached, maybe mildly alarmed. Jonas wonders at himself. (And we wonder, too. Why tell a story like this, twisting and embellishing facts? Had it really been Mary who'd run up the stairs and broken the glass, or had it been you?) He doesn't know Mercer from a hole in the ground. Perhaps the pain in his leg and the Percocet he grubbed from the doctor have loosened the wires in his brain.

Before parting ways, Mercer insists they exchange numbers and emails. He wants to stay in touch.

Two weeks later they meet at a café. It is spring in the City of Gardens and pollen has coated all the outdoor tables and chairs with a sickly yellow sheen, which reminds Jonas of his own nicotine-stained fingers. He smokes in spite or maybe because of this, feeling slightly uneasy, as if he's about to be scammed, or recruited into something he doesn't quite understand.

When Jonas exhales he feels as if he is himself being blown away on the blue cloud of smoke.

How Mercer grins! He has been thinking of Jonas apparently, which is why he has brought a finger-sized nugget of green jade containing what he calls a "Tlingit healing spell." The stone, explains Mercer, has been prayed over, bathed in the light of a full moon, and so enchanted. "Consider this as a gift," he says with a squint and slightly raised chin, "from the ancestors to you."

Ancestors? Who, wonders Jonas, *has Mercer become? And what does* Tlingit *mean? Some New Age thing?*

Taking the small stone, Jonas weighs it in his hand, and perhaps he imagines something there, as if warmth could be felt beneath a cool surface. Once again Mercer is dressed for some gala event for the famously eccentric — he even sports a walking stick made of dark wood and capped with an onyx raven's head — and his eyes seem to laugh from far within an arctic gravitas of knowing.

One month later, Jonas discovers on Facebook that Mercer has walked through a Mercer-shaped hole in the world and is dead.

After emailing an old classmate, Jonas learns that Mercer was found hanging by the neck from a tree in his backyard. No note, just empty beer cans strewn over the lawn. But Jonas gets the message. He knows the tree is significant. Mercer had mentioned it at the café.

Not only had Mercer placed Jonas's green stone at the foot of this tree for its moon bath, but Mercer had gone on to claim that the tree, an oriental plane, was sacred, having been grafted from the original Tree of Hippocrates. "Imagine," Mercer had implored, ever-smilingly, "those same leafy boughs once shaded the father of medicine himself as he lectured his pupils, transmitting some of the earliest wisdom on the modern art of healing."

Jonas figures *Tlingit* must be Greek.

Scar

Jonas, your story is about a failed quest for stable forms of information — and about discovering failure as the purpose of your quest.

There are both falsehoods and truths you begin but forget how to tell — omitted chapters, missing links, dangling threads, obscured figures, clandestine forms, and coded messages from the past imperfect tense —

For example, what about your mother, whose shadow once chased the light around dust-coloured stalks of wheat, whose adolescent sins are still hiding behind the haycocks of the Centre-du-Québec? What about her violin case which, left open, once filled with mating crickets?

Who cares. Today you can have everything you want — scorpion-coloured cigarettes, five hundred flavours of feelings — just nothing you actually need to survive.

It's true, you have the Internet for a brain. A lonely question mark, you go drifting through a world of proclaimed facts.

Having patched together countless swaths of pillaged material, you wear your fabricated outlook like an overcoat, making yourself appear solid, as if you actually possessed a singular and stable identity.

Sure, you can lisp in three mysterious idioms, but your words, blue and trembling, are not your real words.

Thus you secretly perceive the *intrinsic* world as *legitimate*.

Such is the skill of the magician, the professor, the writer, the idiot, the politician. In their trust, the future *loves thee better after death.*

Do you believe that enough information, once gathered and incorporated, might one day crystallize into wisdom — or slow-fade into the image of ashen hands upon ashen sheets, that last day at the hospice?

Do you wonder if the total gravitational force of all your discrete ideas and stored facts will be enough to pull everything together into a monolithic pillar of knowledge — something fixed, rooted, eternal, despotic?

Thinking of those walrus-moustached men of yore — forefathers, heralds, mentors — are they not just cloud-shapes projected through the lens of your nostalgia?

There must be a clearing, a blowout sale followed by a demolition, a raw open space, a brownfield of pure amorality. There must be a war on complacency, something to stew the scum off the insides of arteries, and a constant revolt against bourgeois tropes.

Or the ecclesiastical volutes of cigarette smoke your thinking aspires to!

There must be, in the apple tree, a hummingbird stultified by the rumble and boom of the ultimate space shuttle launch.

Six months heavy with you, inside the bonfire of another August drought, the trapped air clapping with locust wings, let's say your mother stooped to ponder a snakeskin coiled beside a road covered in fine white silt, the "o" of her open mouth, a silent whole note — knowing you'd be born too soon, and not for her, but for the harvest.

Milton, your father argued, was of the devil's party and *knew* it!

Or the flower of a wound, where the closed scar will be the only lasting thing, a testament to *the breath, smiles, tears, of all your life...*

Lab Notes

It would appear that Subject X's overreaction to the news is about as frequent as its being underwhelmed or disappointed, and that its post-9/11 continuation of pre-9/11 aberrant behaviours is about as frequent as its post-9/11 attendance of doomsday-themed social events. However, there may be a problem with our equipment, as the hamsters with their many spinning wheels that power the autoclaves have all come down with the mange.

The Pigeon

A pear-shaped pigeon flashes its unctuous, royally iridescent neck in the sun as it peck-peck-pecks at who knows what stuck in the gum-riddled, sun-bleached, rain-sluiced, frost-cracked, grit-cratered sidewalk.

Wanting to communicate, to soothe and engage with this not-so-*otherly* living thing, Jonas intones, "Yo, *pigeon*!" thinking that his benevolent voice and gentle nature will be enough to persuade this feathery denizen of the street's detritus to act less like a pigeon and more like a friend.

Perhaps they will share a moment of interspecies empathy, their identities shifting, crossing boundaries. For just a millisecond, alive to the thrill of a past life connection, perhaps bird-shape and Jonas-shape will drop their respective facades and twinkle at each other, nakedly, knowingly, as equals.

But at the sound of Jonas's "Yo, *pigeon*!" the pigeon flap-flap-flaps away to perch huffily on a plastic trash bin across the street. Its eyes specks of petroleum. *So like a pigeon*, Jonas thinks and carries on, his legs scissoring over the sidewalk whose wounded surface displays the pronouncement, "FUCK PIGS" next to an equation of love, "CH + MM 4EVR."

Jonas is walking, looking down, beyond his feet, and he is thinking: *shadow canvas, protean sky's stillborn twin, downright, unmoving* — his human heart so often wrong, and hardening.

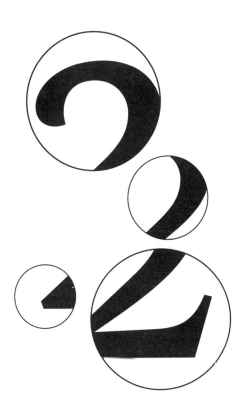

New York

This is the question: where to be? Perhaps Jonas escapes from Victoria and heads to Alfacar, Spain, for a summer, where he tries and fails to find Lorca's grave. Or maybe he trades rainy Vancouver for the Sunshine Coast where the life of the mind inside a driftwood fort threatens to bore him to tears, so he moves to New York and pretends another existence.

Now thirty-something, he suffers from vertigo, agoraphobia, and temporal hiccups. At some point in the future he will live only in the past, just like today.

Surprisingly, people at first seem friendly in New York —unless paid to be helpful, and then they are mean. He finds it is safe to look strangers in the eye, just long enough to take whatever he needs. When his subway car jostles or swerves through a curve, emitting its singular shriek, he knows it is the viola from his favourite Velvet Underground song he is hearing.

In the dank and dripping Chambers Street station, a middle-aged woman, wearing a pink knit sweater for pants sits by the stairs and rocks her torso to her own plangent chanting: "Don't let Satan touch ya *body*. Don't let Satan touch ya *body*..."

By Grand Central Station he breaks down and ingests an ecstasy tablet. The clouds dissolve and the skyline shifts through its various geometric patterns and shapes. In his dream, half of Manhattan is dull firebrick red and the other is grey and resembles the East River if the East River were crystallized iodine. Down by the East River, even though he's rolling, he breaks down and weeps.

But he can't afford to live in Manhattan, so he forages through Brooklyn, where he can't afford to live in Brooklyn Heights, Carroll Gardens, Park Slope, Cobble Hill, the north or east parts of Williamsburg, or a thousand other such places, so he settles in Williamsburg's Southside, *Los Sures*, east of the BQE, which reminds him of parts of East Harlem, though he's never been to East Harlem, except passing through once on the train on his way to the Bronx Zoo, so what does he know?

At home at last in his microscopic third-level walk-up apartment, he observes how the light floods across the ceiling and drips onto the backs of his hands as they grip the worn headrest of the red leather recliner he has just dragged up from the alley. He stretches out his lower back, tilting his shoulders, his hips moving goofily. Even though his windows are shut, music from the street constantly blares through — salsa tunes playing on car stereos, trumpets and tenor voices searching through a longing where Jonas has learned some of the words but none of the meaning.

He begins to sway back and forth. Closing his eyes, he takes stock...

He has begun to suspect that his neighbours regard him as the face of gentrification. *Here I am on the other side of the tracks, the fence, or whatever it is that divides us*, Jonas often thinks while walking the streets, noting the sour looks wafting from the squint-eyed old men stationed, totemic, on every corner of every block. Day after day, the gold and black clad Latin Kings hanging outside the bodega eyeball him, and he can't help noticing how the same Hasidic Jew guns the engine of his big yellow school bus and charges the light every time Jonas tries to cross South Third Street. He has begun to view this bus-driving Hasidic as a not-so-clandestine ninja assassin. This, he knows, is politically suspect.

What's the difference between salsa and rumba, he wonders, shifting his feet in time, his arms raised, his body cruciform, his shadow swaying on the living room wall…

Forty years back, he might have lived on the Lower East Side with the rats and the poet-punk saints. But everything's changed since the Patti Smith era, the city's grit having spun off like kaleidoscope pixels to pollinate the dust with shiny new dust. New York, she has said, has closed its doors to the young and the struggling. But what does she know?

The scene — so Jonas has gleaned from discussions he's eavesdropped on at various cafés during his visits to the other side of the BQE — eventually fled the Lower East Side and relocated here, just over the Williamsburg Bridge. But today, much of this neighbourhood, to everyone's amazement and horror, is an upscale-hipster Disney version of Bohemia. Now it's better to be in Bed-Stuy, or Bushwick, or any place with a razor-wire, bombed-out aesthetic. "SAVE BROOKLYN!" That's what the t-shirts say.

Always too late, Jonas can never afford what's left once he gets there. Having submitted his thesis on class warfare and chased all the artsy chicks, along with his piss-tanked ambitions, right off the stage, Jonas is no longer young, but he is still struggling. Having reckoned that for every Fifth Avenue apartment with a view of the park there's a block of Section 8 housing, he hopes the Canada Council will reconsider his pleas. Or is it actually possible to survive on stealing bottles of water to sell on the subway?

Maybe he could still beat the rush and hit Berlin before the cosmopolitan class of childish reprobates arrives. He never did make it to Prague. Or is Detroit now the new ground zero? What if Satan has already touched everyone's body, mind, and soul — and there's nothing to do, and nowhere left to go?

He wants to explain to his neighbours, to emphasize the difference between these sanctimonious hipsters and a poor artist who can't afford to live in New York. He'd like to point out that the rumours that the krusty kids slinging embroidered sock creatures on Bedford Avenue are all living on trust funds must be true.

It's also true that Jonas arrived with three second-hand blazers, two pairs of deck shoes, and one porkpie hat a half-size too small. And who but some Luddite Canadian would buy all these second-hand books written by dead

French theorists? Where is his history, his northern nightvision, his thoroughbred lust?

Jonas has read that meaning is crafted through difference, that we must picture ourselves as separate beings and stick nature in a category away from the mind — but what if all difference is an illusion manufactured by those assholes, the corporate elites?

This just in: apparently they are pretending to be about to burn down Wall Street again.

The other question is: who to be?

He lives in America, in the Empire State, though he might move to Kraków and change his name to Nick Adams. His delusions, he figures, could stand to get worse before they get better. He wants to do research, to reread *Das Kapital*, but this time without Reagan, Mulroney, or Thatcher buzzing around — those angry mud wasps who once stung, paralyzed, and laid eggs in everyone's brain. Yes, he now believes in parallel realities and past lives, and is especially fond of the time he slunk as a tomcat hunting squirrels and mice along the cobblestone alleys of Leningrad before it switched back to St. Petersburg...

If only he were Spanish, he might relate to someone nearby, maybe speak with the old Puerto Rican men in their fedoras lingering on their stoops, or hunched over a table of dominoes on any given summery afternoon.

At night, everything goes down in front of the International Barber Shop — the laughter, the fights, the bottles going smash in the street, and the salsa tunes still cranking, triumphant, shrill, cacophonous, nonstop. Jonas thinks that perhaps it was on this very block where salsa music began. But he just doesn't know.

So so so... dancing with his new red recliner, Jonas talks with his shadow until it dissolves into daybreak, and pretends not to be...

There is a knock at the door —

Frank's Place

Who knows how, but Jonas befriends an ex-Montrealer named Frank. Frank copes with his anger by memorizing passages from online sources then dropping them into his arguments and stories to justify his outrage. He reminds Jonas of someone —

They have decided to hang out over a pot of coffee at Frank's place, up in the industrial part of Greenpoint which, Frank soon recites, "is part of New York's 12th Congressional District and served by the NYPD's 94th Precinct."

Bearded, with mean hazel eyes, his brow tense and forming a deep vertical cleft above the bridge of his nose, Frank seems to possess a monomaniacal focus of attention, and for a minute he looks just like Jonas's father, only slightly less crazed.

Sitting up in his beanbag chair and narrowing his gaze above a steaming "THIS IS WHAT A FEMINIST LOOKS LIKE" coffee cup, Frank hisses, "But it's really the Russian Mafia, the goddamn *Bratva*, who own this block!"

Jonas conjectures and surmises. He infers, intuits, and concludes that there is a tacit understanding among men that real men must discuss, with much earnestness and grit, only the most consequential of issues. Jonas feels queasy, his stomach an acidic pit, but thinks: *I am Iron John! Let the bonding begin!*

Jonas's first thought is to tell the truth, but he strikes this down and begins to lie, explaining how he was once a bit-part actor before he hit the poker circuit and lost everything — not on poker but on bad stocks.

Frank interrupts. "Mark my words, there's gonna be a war with Iran!" Then his eyes shift slightly as he settles with a slight crunching back into his beanbag, his speech slowing as if he is reading something on the wall just behind Jonas's left shoulder. "Obama will bomb Iran because it's politically advantageous for him. Bush had a ninety-five percent approval rating after the 9/11 attacks. Nobody ever saw anything *like* it."

Jonas continues, saying that ever since the economy tanked he has become obsessed with fifties vibraphone jazz, clove cigarettes, and women with what he likes to call "an ass."

But Frank is now talking about his days playing synth and singing backup in a band called Spalding's Ferry, describing the small towns, the drinking, and the fights with his bandmates in the van on the road. He goes on to list various sets of statistics that convey the idea that the music industry is a pimp for candy-ass pop singers with Jell-O for brains. Jonas imagines Frank frothing at the lips, pounding madly away at his keyboard, and crooning through his square jaw just like some bizarro Kenny Rogers — then Jonas sees his father's face again and forgets what Frank is talking about. Something to do with men not being able to cry?

"My mother was a professional violinist," Jonas half-invents, then stops.

Looking around, he notes the ceiling of Frank's railroad apartment is painted a brassy orange that clashes with the green window and door frames. Local gig posters, mostly of punk bands from the nineties whose members have since either sobered up or died, make a crazy quilt over all the walls. Slouching on a grey leather couch whose cushions are stained with dark mouths, Jonas fidgets and, feeling his bruised hands, has to fight off another barroom flashback. The room smells of ripe cat litter and wet coffee grounds. Light slants though the venetian blinds and plays across Frank's face, making daggers of his oily wisps of bangs.

Charging onwards, Jonas attempts to expound on the topic of money, and the trouble with fiat currency. He explicates how every dollar must be tied to something concrete, like a bullet, or a litre of gas. "But then there's gold, which you can't eat or shoot into your veins. So forget all that speculating, day-trading *bullshit*," he says, feeling himself lapsing into a Porky Pig type of befuddlement. "I mean what exactly is produced by transferring digital figures from one computer to another, other than alienation and m-m-more goddamned d-d-d-d-debt?"

Frank is glaring hard, a Cyclops! He speaks again, but inwardly, just like the Voice: *I say hail comes down, snow from Zeus. The gibbous moon is a thumb of ice. You say there's no such thing? Tell me, in the cold museum of this house, where no one sits to contemplate the view, can feelings still have skin?*

Light claws the orange ceiling. Jonas's knees have begun to shiver. No doubt he needs a pill of some sort, but he has yet to discover one that works for him, for this.

He loses focus and swerves...

When did show and tell become a brass-knuckled attack? All this scheming for an edge, a quip, an insight, a name drop. Nothing offered or conceded. Every pause, a drumbeat; every syllable, a whip.

There can be no alliances, Jonas recalls — only endless skirmishes and these grudges hard as Old Testament stones.

Right then, Jonas invents a new religion, replacing the Son of God with J.D. Salinger, the Devil with Frank, the Church with Solitude, Hell, of course, with Other People, and Paradise with the Power to Become Invisible at Will.

What Jonas needs is somewhere else to go — maybe home, or childhood. He needs an imaginary friend, or someone who will actually *be* there.

He needs more money, a golden bullet, or a great paying career in the literary arts. Perhaps he will pen a weekly advice column, or a comic strip. Why can't his words pay dividends? Why can't he exploit his imaginings for some kind of gain? Or maybe he will write and direct an after-school special while slipping in subliminal messages about the evils of a system based on rivalry and greed.

But thinking of the TV shows he watched as a child — the ones espousing co-operation and brotherly love — he sees them now as a collage of broken glass, where his puppet companions — no longer fun-furred or polka-dotted — go stumbling across the shards...

Vincent, Frank's ancient one-eared cat, comes hobbling over to rub his nose against Jonas's leg. Jonas reaches down but Vincent, his single ear flattened, spits and hooks a claw firmly into Jonas's wrist.

(Because you are so prone to injury and fearful imaginings, the infection will later turn purple and green, resembling the mummified body of a Himalayan bat moth caterpillar invaded by fungus.)

The conversation stops dead — a trickle of blood running from Jonas's wrist like a silent alarm. Frank, waving his "THIS IS WHAT A FEMINIST LOOKS LIKE" mug and sloshing coffee onto his lap, bellows at Vincent-the-one-eared-cat — whose tail is puffed up, and whose back is raised in a triumphal arch at the centre of the room: "*Bad* kitty! *Baaaad*!"

Jonas's breathing catches as his thoughts turn to travelling alone to Madison, Minnesota, where he will either beat drums with or kidnap for ransom that asshole, Robert Bly.

"Thanks for the coffee, I guess," says Jonas, trying his best to contain the oncoming dizziness. "But I think I'll need a tetanus shot."

"The incubation period of tetanus is usually about eight days," says Frank as he rises to refill Jonas's cup with steaming black coffee from a fresh pot.

Afterwards, frowning sarcastically, Frank leans in and softly pats Jonas's back.

Lab Notes

In harmony with our economic inefficiency prophecies — which have materialized, no thanks to all these mechanical whoopsy-daisies — most of Subject X's recurring thought-rashes and existential vacuums have tended to disappear with generous doses of serotonin reuptake inhibitors, and the occasional prostate massage.

Relationship

From next door Jonas hears the frenetically sobbing violins of Vivaldi's "Summer." Although he has yet to formally meet his neighbour, they have passed a few times at the mailboxes in the hall and exchanged nods. He recalls he saw her last summer wearing a wide-brimmed straw hat with a red bow, which he thought was whack.

Now his neighbour's music has infiltrated his cavernous solitude. Jonas intensifies his attention, zeros in, and tries to brush aside the encroaching tentacles of her presence. He needs to write a list, beginning with "Quit your job" and ending with, "Move to a country where landlords do not exist." Only he's stuck on what items might appear in between. Self-improvement classes? Regression therapy? Should he study charm, or Old English? Should he master cunning, or the moribund art of sock-puppetry?

She must have that track on repeat — the same violins keep carrying on, kites swooping in a windstorm.

This has all happened before and will continue happening until finally Jonas decides to take some kind of action — otherwise she's living proof that his will is too diffuse to gather momentum.

Going into his closet, he rummages through a cardboard box of old CDs and removes the Dayglo Abortions's *Stupid World, Stupid Songs* from its cracked jewel case. It is time to ram "I'm My Own God" at the highest amplitude through his busted subwoofer and launch it across the hallway. He'll sink that bitch's battleship, or at least flush her out for some kind of heated exchange in the hallway.

Instead, through a series of awkward apologies and faltering introductions, he makes a friend.

"You're a quirky one," she says bemusedly, one arm thrust akimbo from a tight blue-jeaned hip.

"I'm an artist," explains Jonas, "but today everything's so interdisciplinary and, you know, so multimedia, that it's hard to fit into any one category or form of expression. So what do you, um, you know, do?"

"I used to work at a hair salon," she says, shaking out her curly blonde bob theatrically. "But now I chase down celebs on the streets of Manhattan, and shoot 'em, *bang*, with my trusty Nikon D4. They call me Paparazzo! But my real name is Ursula."

"Well, I'm no one, but my father was kind of famous," says Jonas, trying to keep track of his own words while refusing the urge to ball his hands into fists. "He was this rock star professor of seventeenth-century English literature. He was also a failed poet, and a tyrant. Anyway, he named me Milton, but my friends call me Jay, or John."

"And your mother? What did she — or what *does* she do?"

"My mother? Apparently she was a mute. She died in childbirth. So I came out all... *wrong*."

Two days later they meet under a giant floating Mr. Potato Head at the Macy's Thanksgiving Day Parade. They go to a bar, drink, then back at Jonas's place they fuck and squeal like pigs. Jonas even believes it when she moans, "Almost...almost...almost...yes, I'm *coming*," but then her limbs go rigid as her eyes scrunch shut, and Jonas gets stuck, doubting himself, left in the lurch between pleasure and torment.

Afterwards, as he rolls away, she smacks his bare derrière with her open palm, then, with a "grrrr," she pounces, digs into the flesh of his back with her nails, and bites down hard on his left ass cheek.

At the apex of his scream, just as Ursula's teeth break his skin — Jonas falls in love.

He takes all his previous relationships and crams them into a box, which he fastens with baling twine and mails to Scottsdale, Arizona, with no return address.

He does push-ups and even tries to hoist his chin to the bar in his closet, but the bar slips out of its notches and he spills back into the room in a tangle of hangers, plaid shirts, and houndstooth blazers.

When he closes his eyes he can see Ursula's face shimmering as if it were the residual impression staring at a bright light leaves behind. What she does with blue eyeliner makes little birds cheep inside his chest.

They walk along Avenue D, which once stood for "Death." The air is brisk and bites, and the sky takes on a blister-sheen. Minutes turn to hours and the hours turn to vortices...

She is telling him about her girlhood in Wisconsin, and how she was teased in high school for her breasts, which developed early. Once she was groped...

This is in grade eight. The resident track-star, Mark Berkowitz, and his jock tagalongs approach her as she is opening her locker. Mark reaches in, brutally twists her nipple, and drawls the word "slut" as his friends break out in howls and back slaps.

At first she confides in no one. But after a sleepless night her anger transmutes and she wakes with a determination to act.

"I wanted that fucking asshole prick to suffer consequences," Ursula tells Jonas—and Jonas senses her anger and wonders at how she has carried it this long...

I'm not buying it, is what Mr. Shafter, the principal, says. He goes on to explain how, on the previous day, Mark himself had come to the office to file a lengthy complaint about *her*—claiming that she had been spreading lies about him, telling everyone that he was gay and addicted to steroids.

Ursula listens, her whole body clenched. Once Mr. Shafter has finished, he cocks his head like a challenging bull and widens his eyes. "Well?" he says. Without taking a breath,

Ursula clears Mr. Shafter's desk, sending all of his pens and folders and family portraits clattering, helter-skelter, to the floor.

For this she is suspended, two weeks.

Her mother, a retired social worker perpetually gripped by the prospect of her daughter growing up to become one of the dispossessed, is horrified. Ursula is not only grounded but locked in her room, day and night.

She stops eating, and when she is sent to a doctor who discovers that she has been cutting the insides of her arms and legs with a Lady Bic, Ursula is put into the "psycho ward."

The ward smells of old sweat and mosquito repellent and its bottle-green hallways magnify and echo every cough, sob, and scream. The doctors are scarce and the nurses and orderlies are sadistically blasé. Ursula makes no new friends and refuses to speak in group therapy.

After her first week on the ward, she receives a phone call from someone claiming to be her brother. Ursula has no brother, yet for an instant she believes in the possibility. Perhaps she has had an ally this whole time, a secret sibling, someone rich or maybe even famous who, having caught wind of her unhappy circumstances, has managed to track her down. Not knowing what else to do, Ursula accepts the phone from an unsmiling nurse.

A low male voice breathes one familiar and terrible word, which is followed by hoots in the background. The speaker hangs up — but Ursula gets it. Suddenly it all makes sense. She knows the joke, and how it will go on for a very long time.

Ursula finishes her story as they are sitting down on a bench outside a Turkish café on Clinton Street. And even though Jonas has listened intently — travelling with her into the past, and all the way back again to the present moment — he doesn't understand his role, or what it is she expects of him, or how to react —

"Check it out," Jonas says, pointing down the block at a kid with a Joey Ramone mop and a studded leather jacket patched over with punk insignias and beer logos. "That kid's living the goddamn dream."

The kid is standing midstream of pedestrians, repeatedly lifting an invisible cigarette to his lips in synch to the up and down motion of his bleached-yellow eyebrows. "Punk rock can't die, it won't *quit*," Jonas continues — though Ursula is looking blankly at him now, her story cut off.

Jonas sees this, catches the lethargy of her look, the stalled emotion about to pitch into flat-spin. His three-day beard turns to salt. He clenches his fists and his knuckles become stone, then chalk, then windblown wings of dust.

"Are you cold?" Ursula asks.

But Jonas can't help himself. He is talking and he continues to talk: "God bless the Lower East Side. I wonder if the poets still shoot heroin, if the anarchists still squat. Does anyone protest these days? Conspire? Huff glue? I hope so. That would restore my faith. Did *you* ever rebel? Run away from home to get high and live in the woods? I hear this was once a *badass* place to live, before everyone moved to the land of the Williamsbeard. All this hipster tourism bullshit. Imagine New York in the seventies. You could afford to live here *and* be fucked up on smack. Did you ever hear of the Cobalt in Vancouver? A legendary shithole. Imagine not just a bar but a whole *neighbourhood* like that!"

"I don't really care much about shitholes, or legends," Ursula says, tilting her head to one side and closing her eyes as if something inside her is suddenly aching. "To me, punk was just another macho white-trash fad." *And make no mistake*, Jonas imagines she goes on but without saying it, *you'll always be a tourist, wherever you are, but especially here, no matter how long you stick around.*

They leave and wander uptown. As they are cutting through Stuyvesant Square, Ursula grabs him by the wrist and fast-whispers, "Walk with me one more time around this tree and when we come back, look at that redhead on the bench, the one with the kids over there. You know the actress, Julianne Moore?" Making a gun with her hand Ursula points and hisses, "Shit, if I'd-a brought my camera I could've shot that bitch, *bang bang*."

Later that evening, in Jonas's apartment, they break up arguing about Julianne Moore.

"It was totally *her*!" Ursula growls, making exasperated eyes into her wineglass full of grey tap water. Jonas doesn't believe it. He thinks she is too easily impressed with celebrities.

"Can't you see that part of your consciousness has been hijacked? You're a victim of *make*-believe," he says, feigning calm. "The system's got you trained, and what's worse, you've trained yourself to *be* trained."

(Yes, Jonas, you have figured it all out. You know your own mind, and you feel smug for having outwitted it.)

It's a Darwinian thing. We are pack animals, and our survival depends on moving as one. So there needs to be a guiding force, a nexus of authority that we can all acknowledge and accommodate. The brain, over centuries of trials and errors, and despite whatever dead-end mutations and botched prototypes there have been, the brain, that uniquely specialized instrument of socialization, has been finely tuned, and if it is working, all the pistons firing and the wires properly connected, one of its dedicated functions is to elevate certain citizens above the common fray. Yes, there are those whose delight it is to be lifted above the shifting shadows of mortals, to remind us of immutable truths about ourselves, and to act as the magnetic force around which all of our laws coalesce. These could be moral principles or the rules that govern the discernment of beauty, but they need to be reified, to wear a human face. But celebrities are scammers accessing our program, false gods fabricated by the executive class who play on our greed, fears, and hopes — all for profits that the system feeds on like a dog eats its own shit! All these porn stars with gold watches, these glittering, stupefying, serotonin-jacking images of power and fame administered by elites. It's just a sinister form of palliative care designed to numb the pain of the half-alive populace in order to prevent the kind of full-on agony that might lead to revolt...

(Jonas, ask yourself, were you traumatized as a child? Though you can't recall any violent episodes, something is overtaking you, an antipathy surfacing as this howling steam-engine rush of thoughts pushing the light from the edges of your vision.)

Ursula stays silent. Jonas seems to be talking more to himself now as he paces with his arms rigid at his side. Ursula says nothing — she only knocks her wineglass to the floor where it shatters, then she slams the door as she leaves.

Jonas makes up a reason for each botched relationship. This one he'll claim was ruined by contrary political and musical tastes.

In order to avoid running into her at the mailboxes, he moves back to Vancouver, and then to the Yukon.

Lab Notes

With regard to analyzing its interactions with other subjects, the Overseers have recommended further study of rhesus monkeys alongside the cryptanalysis of Les Enfants Terribles. *And perhaps it is time to revisit ex-covert operative John B. Watson's warning to parents: "When you are tempted to pet your child, remember that mother love is a dangerous instrument."*

Too Far North

As a young man, Jonas can do anything he wants.

(But you're no longer young. Ha!)

So he flees the Desert City, its untold palmettos, plazas, and strip malls. After ditching Oliver beneath a dusty-orange butte just south of Sedona, Jonas continues, on foot…

Or he leaves New York, casting off Ursula and abandoning Frank in his railroad apartment to mutter alone against the fashions and trends, to shuttle unendingly backwards, into the nineties…

Or he departs Vancouver, crossing the steely Fraser River lined by railcars the colour of rust. For a while the countryside flies by, an unfolding series of throwaway vistas, and all he feels is the transient's rush of belonging only to this…

So distance telescopes as he Greyhounds and hitchhikes, travelling north, and further north, finally quitting just beneath the Arctic Circle, to live in a nylon tent tucked away inside a maze of birch…

(Let go. Learn to forget. Never mind the blab of rush-hour philosophy, or the slamming doors of lost opportunities, or the chiming of order bells in the Atlas Bistro of your soul. Here, in this forest, let us suggest that the chalky limbs clacking in the wind are the restless bones of your own ghost.)

Each morning, the rust-pitted George Black Ferry conveys him across the mud-fed Yukon River, and he stumbles into town on dirt roads and uneven boardwalks. This is July in Dawson City. A strange-throated raven is gargling somewhere beneath the ground. Or is it some small demon's dark bubbling of taunts? Or just some lone person weeping?

Nights slip away, star by star, as the lengthening days eat into the darkness. *I'll never die up here*, thinks Jonas to the heavens — drunk for who knows how many days and evanescent twilights, ever since the sun refused to slip beneath the horizon. In this unfamiliar weather, he discovers that he has no need for sleep.

At the Piano Saloon, he plays pool on a scuffed dollar table with Tara. She wears a pink plastic tiara atop an elaborately coiled coiffure, and chain smokes. "Knock it down, you lose," she says, standing a cigarette on its filter end in the centre of the felt.

A hulk of a guy, wearing nothing but a blue tarpaulin haphazardly cinched at his waist by a thin yellow rope, is trying to play "Great Balls of Fire" on the bar's out-of-tune upright piano. He blurts the lyrics in senseless monosyllables: "*Ga-da! Gu-da! Ga ba* dch *·fahya*!"

"Fuck you," says Jonas to no one in particular, leaning over the table and sighting the white along the barrel of his cue. "My generation took video game soundtracks to the dance club and teased golden threads of feeling from basic chemistry."

Tara juts a pointy hip towards the bar, her pool stick hooked under her elbows and running level against the small of her back. Her hands dangle like pale, eyeless, cave-dwelling fish. "My generation aced the exam only to learn that studying to cheat would have been smarter," she says.

Jonas pretends to ignore her, though the image of her angular frame is sketched onto his retinas. And he loves any girl who can leave smudges of cherry-pink lipstick on the rim of a beer mug. And those ghostly hands.

He squints and shoots for the eight, but it bobbles in the corner as the white banks and topples the cigarette. He takes a drink, gets lost for a moment — the half-melted ice cooling his lips, the bourbon burning his throat.

Here, in this place, he can sense each of her words before she speaks them.

"You lose, you pay, you rack 'em," says Tara.

"Fuck that cock shit," replies Jonas. "I'm hang-gliding off the Moosehide Slide and going all the way to Patterson, New Jersey. Baby, let's go!"

In his mind, Jonas tries to put the parts of the story together, but the puzzle pieces are wet and bloated and so nothing fits. He came here, and he left something behind: maybe a friend, maybe his whole life! Or he's been here all along and only dreamt of other selves in other times. Or he has simply drifted into the ever-widening space of summer's north, hoping to find work, hoping absence, hard drinking, and perpetual light might wipe the slate clean.

In this town, where everything seems so familiarly *unreal*, Jonas belongs to everyone but himself, the days blurring without nights, drinking Sour Toes with the German and Japanese tourists at the Eldorado Hotel, Yukon Jack with Tara and the miners at the Piano Saloon, draft beer and bootleg Everclear with the hunters and their Gwich'in guides at the Midnight Sun, then blackouts and waking beside the river, if not delighted at least surprised to be alive, soaked and numb.

Tara is now sitting at the piano, giggling alongside the tarpaulin man, and wiggling her hips. She plucks random keys with one hand while she reaches over with the other to tug playfully at tarpaulin man's rope-belt.

Pale hands, ashen, thin —

"Born to lose! The sun is a goose egg so go suck it, my gold-mining friend!" Jonas shouts, as he sidles up to the side of tarpaulin man, who turns and smashes Jonas in the temple of his melon-sized head. And the lights go bright, then dim...

He'd come across Tara on his second day trudging through town on his way to search for an old classmate he'd heard lived here. Jonas never finds the friend. He meets Tara instead.

Her job is to stand around dressed up in frilly mid-nineteenth-century garb with a wicker basket of purple wildflowers suspended in the crook of her elbow, mugging for the tourists. She catches Jonas's gaze through a throng of camouflaged outdoor adventurist Germans, quickly fluttering her lashes then making her eyes go crossed. For some reason this prompts Jonas to extend his lower jaw and bulge his own eyes in his best Frankenstein grimace. Once the Germans are gone, Jonas lurches towards her with his face frozen in its weird expression, his arms and legs stiffened. He inquires, "Excuse me miss, but how does a monster like me get a job like yours?"

Tilting her head and running her gaze up and down Jonas's spine, she replies, "Sorry kid, but you don't have the ass for it."

Quitting his creature act, Jonas shifts into small talk. "So what brings you this far north? I mean, what are you doing here, my fair lady? Whence didst thou arrive to this place?"

"I'm a sourdough," she declares, "and so I know there are certain questions you just shouldn't ask in this town. The past is a sensitive topic. Or in my case," she says, as she puts one foot behind the other and pinches her ruffled dress in a curtsy, "a gimmick."

Jonas knows he's been asleep his whole life now that he is suddenly awake to discover himself and his surroundings lit from within.

"Well, anyway, I'm Dylan Thomas," he says.

"If you're Dylan Thomas, then I'm Tara, Queen of the Yukon," she replies and then adds, "Hey, do you play pool?"

"I'm probably the best pool player of my generation," answers Jonas.

"Well, I play for money," says Tara, with no trace of irony...

Now a glint of whitewater flashes through the deciduous understory. The rowdy piano tunes have been supplanted by a throbbing in Jonas's head. Windrows of cloud roll across what appears as the floor of the New York Stock Exchange. What is he seeing? Who is looking up at the riverbed, down at the bright-lined sky?

(Contemplate the following questions without attempting to answer: What does isolation mean? Does anyone think of you as anything more than passing through? Jonas, is that really *you*?)

He hears someone breathing his name in the form of a sibilant leaf-sifting breeze. *But I'm Dylan Thomas*, Jonas mouths, unconsciously. Then, through a crosshatch of birch limbs, he notes the first star he's seen in weeks, an unsightly blemish in the milky sky, a pinprick in the idea of forever.

Tara's face is gone as if the season never spun around her oyster-mushroom hairstyle — his gaze never slipping across her bare shoulder where a seahorse tattoo floats above a razor-wire scar.

He'd never even kissed her, had never even tried because he'd known all along the rules of the game, which clearly prohibited any such gestures of unadorned tenderness.

(It would appear that you have been both released and ruined by the discovery that desire is just a contest for survival you are destined to lose.)

Now fall is coming, and Jonas is afraid to travel south, to move alone again, and farther towards the slowly diminishing light.

(So let us take you into the past instead.)

Lab Notes

Questions: Is Subject X's self-awareness program running properly? Are there any micro-tears in the Möbius strip implanted into its proto-consciousness? Its thought process was originally designed as a kind of kinetic sculpture to serve not only as an aesthetic identity-image but also as the bilge pump for the vessel of its so-called spiritual life.

One Year Drifting Backwards and Forwards through Time

As an eighteen-year-old kid, Jonas can do anything he wants.

(Flashback! Ha!)

Instead, he lives in Edmonton, in a clammy basement suite, just off Whyte Avenue, and works at a seafood restaurant washing dishes and sometimes prying oysters from their shells. He likes arranging the grey, amorphous bodies in their leaf-shaped plates, laying them down on a bed of ice with a fancy-pants twist of lemon!

The steam from the Hobart occasionally flares into a rainbow no one notices, until Crazy-Jeff-the-Redhead comes to work one night high on acid and makes everyone stare into the spray.

Jeff is soon fired for huffing whipped cream chargers in the walk-in cooler. Months later, Jonas runs into him at a forest rave on the Sunshine Coast where Jeff, now dressed as a garden gnome, screams above an endlessly looped amen-break that he is engaged to the waitress, Fireweed. "You know, that gap-toothed hottie from the restaurant? Yeah, she's the one I want to stick my dick into for the rest of my life!" Jeff proclaims. Then, nervously swivelling his head, his crazy red dreadlocks swinging around wildly, he searches through all the bodies writhing amid the tall swaying trees, and his pained look confesses that somehow, at this moment, Fireweed is nowhere to be found.

A few months after this — time adrift and churning like chunks of melting river ice — the seafood restaurant's head chef, a blond moustached rocker named Randy — or Lizard, to his staff — appears in a mug shot Jonas is shown at the booking station in an attempt to identify the man who has just robbed Jonas at gunpoint at his new convenience store job in Victoria, BC.

"Déjà vu! That's not the guy, but I know this reptile," Jonas says, pointing towards the image of a Lizard with sad eyes and drooping moustache. "He owes me fifty bucks in tips, and I think he had an affair with my best friend's girlfriend. But working at that restaurant, what could I expect? Arrest him!"

The officer blinks, pushes a dark wisp of hair behind one ear, and turns the page. It seems she dislikes being kidded. "Well, maybe you could quit this job of yours at the corner store, and go back to cooking, but some place better?" she muses.

She's telling him this out of a kindred loneliness, a place where the lightless windows of tenements are the days blacked out on her calendar.

(Imagine how many events are beyond your awareness, and hence your ability to manage or control. For example, this nice officer will soon marry a Dutch magistrate and they will move to Amsterdam where, one cloudless and carefree afternoon, she will notice you panhandling outside the Betty Boop Café. Though your wan face will stand out, she will not be able to place you exactly, stirred by faint pity mixed with a strangely instinctive aversion.)

"Not cooking. Dishwashing," Jonas corrects her…

Every night, after the pots and pans are made spotless, after the flatware, glassware, and silverware are polished and stocked, after the fryer oil has been changed, the floors swept and mopped, and the flattop and broiler scraped clean, Jonas strips off his filthy whites, unties the drenched bandana from his head, wipes his shmegy brow, and splashes cold water over his face.

(Repeat unto death, and later still, from the Kingdom of the Afterlife: the social order is tied with human sinew, and work — especially stultifying work — is a muscle.)

Entering the grotto-dim lounge, he finds Randy sitting on his favourite after-work stool, lizard-eyed, scotch with ice raised in one hand as if to toast the hour, his head bent over the lines of cocaine he has cut up on the bar.

The same Led Zeppelin song always throbs through the room like a toothache — if a toothache were pure pleasure, if pure pleasure were a mix of booze, coke, and minimum-wage sweat. *Maybe there* is *something to this miserable existence*, Jonas sometimes finds himself thinking. (Even though your mind is numb and your spirit aches, can you feel the power swelling in your abdomen? Yes, there are rivers and streams underground. There are invisible currents of dishwater. There is something down there you want to float away on.)

At this hour, Lizard rarely smiles or speaks, just nods and dips his moustache into his glass, his bulleted pupils occasionally transmitting a current of dark feeling. Sure, he is a terrible boss, prone to punching walls, writing bad cheques, and screaming at wait staff. He is a felon of some sort (as has been revealed). He is a seducer of women — or so Jonas suspects though he never tells Jeff. And he is a reptilian drunk who, if provoked, is able to shoot blood from his eyes.

But Jonas still thinks that Lizard is a hell of a guy when it comes to stoically basking in the intoxicating glories of the restaurant industry!

And so it goes, the days and months pouring out, surrounded by eddies of flotsam...

Then one day Randy is nowhere to be found, and neither is the head waitress, Fireweed. Both are gone and no one can explain it. To Jonas these absences suggest the presence of secret portals, and the idea that, at any moment, anyone might vanish only to reappear somewhere else, in some other time or place.

Jonas decides to enter the mystery — he too will go missing — and he stops going to work.

So so so...he moves out west, to the coast, where he is reunited with Jeff, and later, in a driftwood bungalow facing onto a pebbly, kelp-strewn beach, he is re-introduced to the waitress who is now Jeff's three-months-pregnant fiancée. "You remember Jonas, from the restaurant!" Jeff exclaims happily, but Fireweed just looks out across the stony shoreline to the white-blown waves and whistles an eerily pitched note through her teeth.

Rumours of Lizard persist: death by Hell's Angels, death by ex-wife, death by turning to Jesus in a time of distress. And there is a legend of two bullet holes plugged through the door of a Peruvian cathedral...

On Halloween, Jeff and a pumpkin-shaped Fireweed are married in a bar in Gibsons, both of them dressed up as zombies. Soon thereafter they get a divorce — meaning that for all eternity they are each cursed to nurse their drinks at the opposite sides of the same bar in the same beachcomber town. The baby, whose name is Rain, gets passed around.

Meanwhile, a clown-masked man with a sawed-off shotgun levelled above stacks of candy bars and breath mints threatens Jonas's life. For weeks Jonas can't get rid of the words, "The till or I'll blow your guts out!"

Taking the nice police lady's advice, Jonas quits his job as a convenience store clerk.

Finally, poor Crazy Jeff — heartbroken, strung-out but trying to get clean, his head now shaved and scabby — fronts Jonas his whole supply of crystal meth, which Jonas sells to tweekers at Vancouver parties and raves, and makes enough so that he can pay Jeff back and buy a one-way ticket to Amsterdam — a magical city where, according to Jeff, "the drugs are free and the women are sleazy" — his eyes brightening with a faraway gleam...

How Jonas lives! — first in a former insane asylum repurposed as an anarchist squat, then in Vondelpark in a secret tree-fort community nicknamed Windermere. He wafts along the whole summer on waves of hashish and Heineken pilfered from the ass ends of delivery trucks. He turns nineteen in the air, at the highest point below sea level, a mad baron perched above a three-acre cloud-reflecting pond, enshrouded in dreams of lawless freedom, and feeling as if he is being pried open — just like an oyster! — by the beginnings of a spiritual decay.

For money he busks with a ukulele, which he can barely tune and is missing a string and a peg. To compensate for his lack of musicianship, he skips in circles and occasionally leaps and twists theatrically up into the air.

One day, just after he has somehow managed to turn his body a full revolution without his feet touching the ground, he sees, despite his dizzy-stoned brain, a familiar-looking woman — prim button blouse, dark hair tidy in a bun — who drops five guilders into his upturned fez, and hurries off — no eye contact.

Déjà vu! Jonas feels as if he is floating, deliciously alone, as if the city's countless bridges and concentric canals have led him to himself, in this very moment — inexplicably!

That night, nested high inside Windermere's branches, as he is slipping into a swirling, starry sleep — his past sloshing around inside his head — he has the novel idea of writing a novel. He thinks to spit *right-back-atcha!* into the face of existence, to map out all the interconnections and chance encounters of a single year — but without forcing a purpose. *Telling an actual story*, Jonas tells himself, *would be way too bourgeois.*

Then he finds himself wondering about the nice lady — although he doesn't know why — and if she ever caught up with Lizard, and if Lizard still lives…

Factotum

You work as a Walking Sign Board, a Talking Mannequin, a Singing Magician, a Signing Event Coordinator, an Event Horizon, a Youth Hostel Demolition Expert, and a Canine Clairvoyant.

You try many things, and you fail and lose. The leather straps chafe your nipples. Your ballpoint pens go abstract expressionist all over your oxford pinstriped shirts. The mops mildew and rot in the storeroom. After several false starts, your computer attains a state of cryogenic stasis, at one with Walt Disney.

You work as a Breakfast Chef, a Brunch Chief, a Prep Cook, a Dish Pig, a Deck Shoe Salesman, a Sloe Gin Taster, a Prison Wharf Rat, a Toast Monkey, a Shopping Cart Ninja, a Codfish Wrangler, and a Scuba Solicitor.

You place the signage, with spelling errors, above the escape hatch instead of the washroom. Dropping your wand, coins spill from your sleeve, not only revealing the gimmick, but exposing your kleptomaniac bent. On your first and only tour you are kidnapped by Dutch extremists.

You work as a Convenience Store Jerk, a Database Canvasser, a Clark Kent Impersonator, a Class Clown Tutor, a Sales and Marketing Enrichment Assessor, and a Field Hockey Practice Mooch.

You dream your order wheel is a spinning carnival ride, each ticket a screaming child whose mouth bleeds the yellow goop of yolks broken in the pan. The toast burns and smells of the underside of a polluted creek in Winnipeg. Once again, the bellicose waitresses in beehives and horn-rims make you polish the silverware. They make you do the cashout, which doesn't add up because everyone's income is down the barroom pisser. Someone wants their coffee harder than granite, their steak black with extra cracked marbles, and a side of photocopier toner.

You work as a Dessert Technician, an Executive Grouch, a Twenty-Four-Hour Maintenance Robot, a Diesel Maniac, an Assistant Mangler, a Skilled Labradorite, an Internet Dentist, a Crooked Line Cook at the Gorilla Griller, a Bastard Barista, a Bebop Critic, a Child Catering Blog Contributor, and a Porn Copywriting Poet.

You quit your job and leave town, a self-projected figment of Paul Newman's ghost. Lighting a stagy cigarette, you hitchhike south, alone. You haven't been home in years. The money you've salvaged burns a hole, first in your pocket, then in your self-esteem. Your looks turn cartoonish. You have nothing to eat yet your boots are caked with the detritus and muck of leisurely appetites, and your clothes reek of the kelpy shore where the heiress of your misspent youth still lives in her nineteenth-century dotage.

Your mind's not right.

Fired for losing your temper. Let go for producing another primetime failure. Convicted for forging your own identity. Caught cheating at teaching again. What's worse, your students' parents are plugged into the Herman Melville Appreciation League which manages the Human Resource Department at the Online Mid-Life Crisis University.

You fall out of the loop, and out of favour, and land cheek first on the bloodstained concrete. Blacklisted, shunned, starved for affection, your game-face hinges on a disdain disguised as competence. Desperate, you take an income-tax origami workshop as a pre-emptive strike against drug rehab zealots. But the Student Loan Officer has tapped your phone and you can hear his breathing and see his dark face in every moonlit tree.

The power is turned off, and so is the oxygen.

In the Social Assistance Torture Chamber, when the receptionist gives you the number 565 on a blue slip of paper, you break open and cry. And from your tear ducts spill pearls and diamonds which fall to the ground and grow to the size of James Franco's head, and from your throat streams of liquid gold flood the room and everyone is floating away, the shower-capped hustlers, the invidious surgeons, the prize-less rhymesters, the shoeless would-be ushers, and the lonely owners of home insurance policies set to expire next week — all of them rise on your outsized self-sorrow, and drift towards the waffle-coloured ceiling where all are equal in the convergence of unmet desires.

You can't spell. You can't exhale or speak *properly*. Inhibited, you never know how to stand, or what to do with your lips, especially when listening to that avant-gardist in Bolshevik garb who constantly flouts his MacArthur Fellowship — at such times you stare with a Gnostic intensity at the air's invisible circuitry.

Your fingers, you're convinced, are the wrong size for your hands, which you unconsciously ball into fists every time it's your turn to ask your imaginary parole officer's stepdaughter to dance.

Your ears stick out like the handles of a moped!

To study the art of body language, but to fail the exam. To research your options, to option your scripts, then to go nodding off as the movie begins. At job interviews and speed dating encounters alike, to attempt to regale the other with displays of out-of-date jargon, and to flaunt the trinkets and talismans of ideologies that long ago went down with the ship.

Sentimental about your own precious feelings, you nurture a nostalgia for people and places you've never known or seen, yet the purpose of your wanderings is to steel yourself against wistfulness and longing. You wish you could play the vibes, or maybe the zither, and wonder why no one will pay you for your creativity — so what if your filigreed ice cubes always melt before anyone can see your intricate designs?

It was your parents' generation that told you — by way of history warped by money, dry martinis laced with pure LSD, and access to tenure-track sinecures — that you were special, that you could play the ukulele if that's what you wanted, that the gift of a singular passion was all you needed to thrive in the happily spoiled First of all Worlds.

Your kingdom for an arts grant! Your project involves painting all your neighbourhood fire hydrants into the likenesses of robots and spaceships. You're full of ideas, though these days you mostly stay at home practising card magic, watching funny cat videos, eating raw Mr. Noodles, and calmed by the fact that everyone hangs on — toiling away, madly, blindly — but no one survives.

Lab Notes

Because of the philosophical system already embedded in its DNA, Subject X can say "in the Aristotelian sense" about almost anything. As such, Subject X remains oblivious to our existence, not to mention preoccupied with laughing at its own cleverishness.

Back in the City of Broken Glass

Having matured and mellowed with age, and having crawled up through the bowels of the restaurant industry, Jonas not only washes dishes, but he now cooks short orders. Cramped into the bar's airless kitchen, skating around on the greased linoleum, wielding honed French knives and hot saucepans, Jonas works blissfully alone. He sees himself as a failing freak-show act. Or no, he is Mayakovsky stuck inside a fisheye lens. Or no, he is a one-man crew of a rattrap submarine, Captain Nemo without a clue!

He is stable for once, he is sober, but chits are piling up: chicken parmesan, bruschetta, popcorn shrimp, nachos, and three poutines.

Beyond the swinging doors, bathed in the endless radiance of televised hockey highlights, the pub's regulars — middle-aged, corpulent, fish-eyed lumps — hunch over their cheap mugs of foamy yellow beer, sinking silently inside themselves. Jonas knows this journey, the brain descending, the chin delving into the dark waters of the solar plexus. He knows this partially submerged place, opaque with nostalgia and slimy with regrets. He knows how lonely Vancouver can be in the fall, winter, and spring.

He sears the chicken, dunks a basket full of shrimp into the fryer oil, layers the nachos with cheese for the microwave, then stuffs the bruschetta in the Salamander to broil, all the while thinking that in another world, anything might happen. Some other kitchen could be skimming beneath the waves, the dishwasher squelching and pinging its way along the sea floor's topography — while here, in this greasy and muggy corner of a Friday evening, his machine, his sturdy Hobart, can only chug and wheeze along, fulfilling its function, sterilizing the silverware, beer mugs, and plates.

Nevertheless, he stands firm, feet planted on the (caution: slippery!) linoleum, employee of the hour, the centre of all things, paragon of kitchen helpers, clothed in diaphanous shreds of steam, slightly lost in the clutter of his half-thoughts. Oh, yes, he is a responsible, wage-earning, tax-paying, workaday citizen and necessary component of if not a flourishing then at least a *functioning* commercial enterprise. He has a weekly schedule: two till closing, Wednesday through Saturday; and daily responsibilities: cook, prep, wash dishes, take stock, mop. Bad-luck to whoever bothered to build the pyramids, or write a brief history of the short-lived, or invent the microchip — suckers and dupes. Jonas, king of his domain, sovereign of the here and now, gets fountain drinks for free and sometimes calculates his own tips! Indeed, there is a financial value given to his labour and time — or so he tells himself, to defend his position, to explain why he's stuck scuttling around with the cockroaches and mice, instead of out there, getting wrecked with the bloated and blurry lumpenproletariat.

He has forgotten to sprinkle diced olives over the nachos again. Examining the jar, where a straw-hatted man wearing green overalls and bearing a wooden bucket climbs a ladder up into the foliage of a tree whose sunlit limbs tangle and combine to spell the word "*ITALIA*," Jonas wants to tell the man that the existence of a short-order cook, like a poet's or a painter's or a puppeteer's, is not what it appears to be, not an exercise in self-defeat, but a kind of conceptual artwork, the high-irony of a lifetime devoted to the pursuit of internal rather than external goods. What worldly careers can compare to the treasures of a rich inner life, other than, perhaps, olive picking in Tuscany?

He has forgotten to drop the fries for the three orders of poutine — goddamn it all, and shit-fuck. Every stupid mistake he makes delays his one reward of smoking half a Belmont Mild in the back alley, motherland of yowling cats, green garbage dumpsters, and a pure infinitude of chilly night air that turns his breath to Russian ghosts...

Earlier that day, walking to work on sidewalks dotted with cigarette butts, pigeon shit, bottle shards, and new spots of rain, Jonas was convinced that his life in the city would never change. But later this evening, the event that will chart the course of his summer, the incident that will transport him to the desert and present him to the luminous beings who possess the secret knowledge of how to travel backwards in time, occurs near closing, when Jonas forgets to warn the new gangly limbed waitress, Martha, that he has just mopped the kitchen floor.

At a quarter to midnight, his shift almost done, Jonas watches with paralyzed panic as Martha, after having kicked open the kitchen door with the tip of her black Mary Jane, comes rushing in, a tray of dirty mugs balanced in each hand — then her feet slipping out from under her, her elongated arms tossed heavenwards, and her torso tilting madly as if she is sliding into home plate. There is a black and white explosion as legs arms trays mugs and the steel prep table combine, fall apart, then come crashing down.

Snapshot: a crimson rivulet forever investigates the cracks in the linoleum tiles around Martha's opened forearm.

(Here it is, the motif that will haunt you through the years: a mosaic of broken glass, and the echoing blood you cannot make cohere.)

Your fault! says the Voice.

"So sorry. Fuck! So sorry so sorry," says Jonas, clenching and unclenching his hands, stepping towards her then turning away, not sure whether to pull her to her feet or dash outside for help. Whatever it is that jolts life along from point A to point B is failing him again. "There is some kind of first-aid kit?" says Martha nonchalantly, shock making her voice sound relaxed, her face almost exultant as she clutches her bleeding arm, holding it up like a trophy, one strap of her black dress nestling in the crook of her elbow. "Oh, yes," Jonas says, then sprints to the back office where in the corner next to the mop he finds an old sour cream bucket whose contents include an empty soft pack of Players cigarettes, a pink lighter, a red kidney bean, a latex glove, a tube of Neosporin, and a tattered roll of surgical gauze. "Here it is!" he cries out. "Help is on the way!"

Seated on a slumping box of potatoes, Martha lifts the strap of her dress, closes her eyes, and mutely proffers her arm. As gingerly as he can Jonas grips Martha's wrist, noting her frosty pink nails before he slowly turns her palm supine and, mustering his determination, inspects her inner forearm. There is a deep puncture hole, but the bleeding slows and Martha hardly flinches as Jonas smudges the oozing tip of the Neosporin tube around the wound, then wraps her limb in several layers of gauze, depleting the roll. Lacking tape he ties everything up with butcher's twine, which he cuts wrenchingly with a paring knife.

"There you are. I have made you whole again," Jonas says, and tries to smile. Martha's eyes, he sees, are rimmed in pink and her mascara has clotted at the tips of her lashes.

"Your hands are trembling," she remarks quietly with what Jonas fears might be a trace of scorn.

"I'm okay. I'll be just fine, thanks," Jonas says, then inwardly winces — then faints...

The next day, lying on his back beneath his bedcovers, staring up at the pattern of cracks in the stucco ceiling, a pillow clutched tightly to his chest, Jonas shivers and aches. It is one o'clock and he is scheduled to be back at work in an hour, but he feels feverish. He is still struggling with his dream of last night, unable to square his words with his behaviour. If he could at least grasp his language at a point close enough to its origins in order to confront his fucked-up emotions... Instead he hears the Voice: *Lack of accountability! Failure of foresight! Incompetent! Slacker! Escapist!* Why did his hands tremble? O cursèd extremities! Why did he say and do what he said and did? He should have given Martha his share of the tips. Her bandaged arm, he now sees, resembled a mummy's ragged appendage. And what kind of man gets dizzy spells? Who *swoons*?

But it is late spring, and the sun — suddenly streaming through a hole in the clouds and splintering through the dense crowns of holly trees outside Jonas's bedroom window — has begun to show signs of caring again, casting an arabesque onto the thin comforter and warming Jonas's quivering legs.

He makes a decision.

At two o'clock, he turns off his phone then brews a pot of Irish tea, which he drinks with honey seated at his kitchen window. Observing a congregation of small birds niggling and jostling one another along the length of his neighbour's wrought-iron fence, Jonas holds the thought that the cities in which he so often finds himself can only breed small-mindedness and contempt. If his life is to be unique or interesting, it must exist in opposition to how the world expects him to behave. The equivalent of personal integrity, decides Jonas, is to be answerable to no one. True vision is nothing less than radical inwardness.

He spends the rest of the afternoon shuffling around the kitchen in his boxer shorts, mumbling to himself and flicking cigarette ashes into the sink. In the evening he goes on the Internet and learns that swooning is also called lipothymia, then searches for information about how to work for food and lodgings on organic orchards on the Mediterranean coast.

Finally, he goes out drinking to celebrate the end of his money, and winds up in jail.

Lab Notes

Future experiments could involve the following: the introduction of 1) sudden male pattern baldness in conjunction with high levels of sports trivia; 2) random inflictions of pain whose source remains hidden; 3) sudden bursts of euphoria whose source remains hidden; 4) a visceral experience of Heidegger's concept of "unconcealedness" reversely propitiate in intensity and quality to Subject X's intellectual understanding of the same.

Gymnastics

The day you come home, you lose your sense of identity, your sense of direction…

Late February, the afternoon light passes through a rusty sieve of bare branches and trickles over the linoleum floor you are pacing. After a dark and stormy night, and terrible Mr. Noodles dreams, you feel as if the whole mad world is lapping up against your apartment window. Troubles, wanting in.

Déjà vu, but the boring kind, stuck in a loop, different city, same Nowhere, just where you started.

No doubt your neighbours are paying off mortgages, inventing yoga schedule spreadsheets, and transforming their guest rooms into nurseries for triplets. But your energies swirl in your head.

How many times can you pretend to be about to start to read *Ulysses*?

You'd call Oliver, but Oliver is at another UFO conference in the desert. You'd call Frank, but for weeks Frank has been incommunicado, presumably holed up in a funk of self-loathing ever since his new band, The Whistling Prix, having reached a consensus on their own lack of interest, broke up. Crazy Jeff, alas, is back in the psych ward after having been pinched by the fuzz for threatening to throw himself from the Burrard Street Bridge.

You write in your Relaxation Journal "Inertia, thy name is Jonas!" then think: *time to get busy*, and start to draft a poem entitled "Ode to Voodoo Stick Pins," getting as far as

> Voodoo Stick Pins Voodoo Stick Pins
> I like the socks that cover your shins

then giving up poetry forever.

Last month, your old high school burned down, or was it last year? Apparently you are old enough to have forgotten whatever it was you were trying to remember. Your mother's birthday? Your own age?

If there is a purpose to any of this it must be simply to continue without a purpose, to endure not only hardships but the widening fissures of these drab and artless hours when the day's regrets suck the light from the corners of the room.

I'm a sad sack! you think, engrossed in yourself as one who tenderly prods a bruise.

You nod off, seated at the desk. As always, cars swish by on streets now become rivers in the rain that falls with dusk — rain wanting to tell you things, tap-tapping you back awake.

Rising from your chair, groggy, you light a cigarette and, exhaling the first drag with a sigh, you envision a bridge built from stones whose wet surfaces once serialized the river's endless news.

Next, the specks that constitute your identity you imagine as grains in a photograph entitled "Another Portrait of the Colour Grey."

Jonas, whoever you are, you sing to yourself, *you are merely trafficking in images and sounds, crossing the darkly flexing spaces in between!* Flicking the orange cigarette ash into a tin can, you see the cities of the world decimated by an atomic catastrophe.

Maybe *this* city's to blame — how it wants to ruin you, so full it is with the white powders you know you could get your hands on with one last paycheque and a phone call. You could turn your nerve endings into flashing Christmas lights just one more time to ease you through this endless transition.

You've been here too long, with no means of escape. But maybe you could still hook an existential thread, unravel the fabric of your ache, and have some new material with which to begin again — as an MFA creative-writing student?

It's time you fell in love (but *this* time) with a real human being!

You need some kind of force to push against, the slow disaster of a new obsession — otherwise this is all gymnastics on the moon.

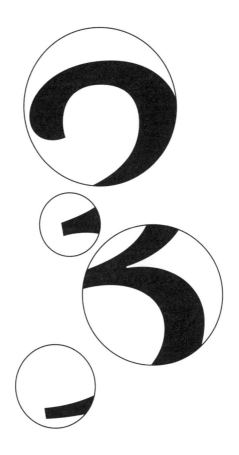

Mr. Sock

The eyeless mannequins, with their up-to-the-minute fabrics and motifs, have lured a huge, white, middle-aged, middle-class mob from the streets! Jonas, on a manic upswing, wants to merge, to enter the stream. Every aisle is awash with wan faces.

This could be anywhere in America, thinks Jonas, not remembering where he is.

Sweater vests are flying off the racks like angels in distress, whispers a sales clerk to the make-believe companion inside Jonas's head. But Jonas knows the game. There are cameras and speakers hidden in the false ceilings.

A tinny voice cuts in on a drum-and-bass version of "Jingle Bells" with the announcement: *Dear Christmas shoppers, long live fleecy jackets, earmuffs, and plaid winter skulls — uh, scarves!*

The store greeter is a lanky man with a pencil moustache and one droopy eyelid. Jonas tries communicating, using a sort of sign language he invents on the spot: *Flawed is better than perfect, don't you think?* he gesture-speaks, rolling his shoulders and shuddering his hips. *It's mutations that drive the economy — all those bent little sprigs shooting off in odd directions — and not the continual submission to traditional* standards.

"The discount items are in the back," says the greeter, his wonky eyelid quivering slightly like a moth's injured wing. "Right behind the Christmas tree hat rack."

After trying on several fedoras and paperboy hats all too small for his frowzy-haired melon, Jonas is drawn to a row of cylindrical bins, each one full of argyle socks. He crowds in with the other shoppers rummaging and digging around. "I'm looking for Mr. Sock, the perfect puppet-friend," he says, accidently elbowing a woman in the fat of her breast. Her gaze narrows menacingly as she turns and holds a sock up to the light as if it were an envelope whose contents she hoped to espy. *Pardon me*, Jonas says, wiggle-waltzing, *but did you know that nature is a limited human construct? The seasons and tides can't always be predicted. Any day now, the magnetic poles might flip!*

But the woman is gone, and in her place a giant security guard stands, staring ahead, Easter Island statue-like. Jonas tosses a sock back into the sea of jumbled textiles. "Be free! Swim with your own kind!" he screams.

Later, in an airless room congested with video monitors, winking switchboards, and several cardboard boxes marked "LOST & FOUND," Jonas finds himself seated in a metal chair, his vibrating hands tucked under his thighs. He is wondering how to explain to the rent-a-cop, who sits at the other end of a cluttered card table, the ultimate inconsequence of shoplifting a single argyle sock.

No one speaks, yet Jonas is sure he can hear words at the periphery of his earshot. Yes, there is a voice coming from the slanting row of dog-eared books sticking out from the box next to Jonas's feet. Then Jonas sees it: wedged between the spines of an *Introduction to the Philosophy of Ethics* textbook and a copy of *Franny and Zooey*, a tiny one-eyed doll's head is crying out for help.

The cop rises and belches softly into his cupped palm while staring intently at a red push-button telephone mounted on the wall beside the only door. He eyes the phone as if at any moment a call might come to relieve his gastronomic distress.

Quickly Jonas reaches down, plucks out the little head, and tucks it inside his shirt's front pocket.

Look, Jonas whispers to the little head, *I'll say it all again. Mittens are for kittens, and flawed is better than perfect. Leave the exquisitely formed to the eighteenth century.* The guard switches hands and now his burps are more audible, coming out in a rapid succession of diaphragm-quivering upsurges. With his other hand he clutches the leather belt that struggles to contain his distending gut.

Leaving his seat, Jonas jogs over to a counter where he tries bending the metal stem of a small microphone into the arc of a swan's neck. "No no no," says the guard, now seemingly paralyzed as he holds onto his belt with two hands — a drunken captain on rough seas — his feet anchored and his torso slightly swaying.

Jonas taps the mic before trying to speak to the shoppers whose grey shapes are flickering inside a small monitor. *Dear mutants! Every generation reads Shakespeare differently. His dark one wears the face of the times!* But the shoppers continue, deaf, oblivious, their progress captured in a stuttering series of jump cuts. It appears that something or some*one* is removing segments from their lives, and now only frames — isolate, disjointed — remain.

His sock, Jonas notices, is hanging like a small animal skin from a hook mounted on the counter's lip.

"Sit down. Do not. Do not. Touch," stammers the guard, between throaty explosions. Then his body seems to deflate suddenly as he slumps back into his chair and closes his eyes.

Whirling around Jonas addresses his captor, singing his words to the opening bars of "Frosty the Snowman": "Heeeeey, Mr. Square Pants!" Switching idioms, Jonas goes on in a mechanical vein: *Danger Will Robinson! We must anticipate failure and include it as part of the American dream! Dust to dust! Radical humility must shield us! There's nowhere to fall, nowhere to go but further into the machine!*

The red phone buzzes, making one of its little lights blink. Yet the guard doesn't stir. His skin has turned the colour of skim milk. He opens his eyes to slits.

But Jonas is in the zone. He can't stop robot-dancing. And as he jerks his torso back and forth, the tiny doll's head drops from his pocket and skitters across the floor, halting at the guard's polished boot tip — where it screams and screams and screams...

The red phone continues to buzz and to blink, a star trying to go nova. The guard looks down at the floor, looks into the doll's tiny blue eye, and manages to say weakly, "Get out of here, kid. And. Don't. Ever come back —"

Jonas leaves the doll's head behind, but snatches Mr. Sock from the hook before moonwalking out.

Self-Diagnosis

It starts with a slight tingling on the right at the base of his skull, and then turns to an itch, which soon deepens and establishes itself as dull pain. As the hour passes, the left side of his head mimics this same sequence of sensations. Next, the disease becomes a rash that spreads up behind both his ears and pools at his temples which, Jonas sees with a start in the mirror, have turned a brighter shade of scarlet.

Lying down on his couch, with only his sock puppet for a friend, Jonas touches the back of one hand to his head in a repose of mannerist distress, looks at his other hand, argyle clad, and says, "Mr. Sock, I think this is it."

He is supposed to be writing today, short introductions to online porn clips, for which he gets paid two cents a word.

"Don't be a dreamer. This isn't science fiction. Money makes *money*," Jonas's faceless boss tells him, calling from Miami Beach. "And sex is what *makes* money make money which, as I already *know* you know, makes the whole fuckin' world go 'round!"

"Porn makes nothing happen," replies Jonas, but his boss has already hung up.

The trick is to front load the descriptions with appropriate key words in order to optimize search engine results*: missionary; doggy style; double reverse cowgirl; 360 bigspin to spread-eagle nosegrind,* etc. The setting is important: *in* *the woods; at the office; on a living bearskin rug; in a Catholic reformatory of the unreformed mind,* etc. As are racial labels like: *ebony; ivory; chocolate; vanilla; the best Tex-Mex in Austin,* etc. And certain physical traits like: *hirsute; tribal scars; balloon smuggler; furry yellow come-hithering tail feathers,* etc. In the world of virtual flesh, the combinations and permutations are endless — and Jonas sometimes gets carried away...

But now he feels feverish, somehow aquatic, and when the rash spreads into a mottled headband, his first thought is *meningitis*. His second thought is *cancer of the blood*. His third thought is stillborn, his fishy mind sliding from embryonic darkness and falling earthward, towards inescapable doom.

The situation, Jonas realizes, requires immediate medical attention, or at least an online search. So what a relief it is when, after googling his suspicions, he finds he can touch his chin to his chest, thus ruling out meningitis. The symptoms of the cancers, however — *Hodgkin's disease; leukemia; lymphoma,* etc. — are so varied and complex that he gives up his research and becomes resigned to jerking off, then floating away like a dandelion seed into the depths of the Grand Canyon.

An hour later, the rash has swollen into a pox of blotchy welts and it is growing more and more tender and sore. As energy evacuates his body, Jonas instinctively retreats to the couch again where the imperative is no longer to write concupiscent sketches but to watch cable TV and lose himself in as many quirky romantic comedies as possible.

His favourite is about a male and a female who want to keep their relationship on a superficially sexual level. O glossy exemplars of white heterosexuals! The female, a particle physicist, is pretty and practical, though she likes to win arguments by raising her voice and unleashing assaults of rapid-fire gibberish. The male, an author of children's books, is brutish, dull-witted, and obsessed with what he believes to be his inner life, which involves taking afternoon naps in the nude and sucking his thumb. Due to a botched experiment involving quantum fields, the couple is transported to an alternate universe where they must battle an evil Child Emperor who hoards all the Fun. The male uses his dream journal to defeat the Child, and in the process he loses his dread of the dark while ironically discovering that his female companion possesses certain nurturing attributes to which he had been previously blind. Now that all his misdeeds are magically forgotten, he is compelled to lure the female into marriage, the adoption of twins, and finally, silence.

When the credits begin to scroll, Jonas emits a small sob as his sinuses flood and a tear burns down his cheek. He is shivering, even wrapped in a wool blanket with the heat cranked. His forehead kills.

At midnight, unable to sleep, he checks his supplies and discovers that he will soon inhabit a world without orange juice, chicken soup, ibuprofen, or hope. What's worse is that Jonas has run out of people. Here, in this place — somewhere between Limbo and the Kingdom of the Afterlife — he has no one to call for help. If he dies from this cancer in the night, who, other than Mr. Sock, will even notice he is gone? The tragedy of his life, he decides, lying back down and pulling the blanket up over his head, is that no one has ever loved him for his faults. No one has ever forgiven him.

Doubling the NeoCitran dose, Jonas falls into darkness then awakens somewhere deep within the Black Forest, where an apparition of a young girl emerges from the mist. Dressed in a red-hooded gown, she beckons with one finger to follow. Soon they are inside a cave-gloomy cabin whose only light comes from a fireplace where the blaze appears to be frozen in time and pixelated. The girl takes Jonas's hand. Her face is a shadow inside her red hood. The thought occurs that this is no fairy tale, and the girl, no simple ingenue. Key words write themselves and scroll across Jonas's vision: *red; hot; young; white* — and he begins to lay her over a sheepskin coverlet, drawing her crimson garment away from her chest. There is something beneath her robe, an unexpected surface, nothing like exposed apple-flesh — instead her skin is ruined with dark bruises and sprayed with the tiny red and white pustules of infected needle pricks. Her face dislodges itself and slips away like a cat over the side of the bed.

Jonas starts awake, an iron taste on his tongue, his bedsheets soaked, his body all ice. On the nightstand his phone is vibrating and flashing a number from Miami Beach. Jonas thinks: *hives, shingles, HIV*. The phone skitters to the table's edge and drops. He thinks: *somehow I must deserve this* —

In the Freezing Rain

Jonas is pretending to wait for a friend in front of a methadone clinic in a secret part of San Francisco that reminds him of East Berlin with its litter-strewn sidewalks, ancient graffiti, and cement walls pitted with what appear to be bullet holes. No, wait, it reminds him of Toronto, where every building has been designed for the sole purpose of celebrating the integrity and essential decorum of the ninety-degree angle. This cold rain, of course, signifies death and Seattle.

Across the street, beneath a dripping grey-stained awning, a tattoo-headed teenager sits inside an arterial system of brightly coloured PVC tubing, one end of which he blows into, playing an almost subsonic melody vaguely resembling Nirvana's "Come as You Are." This plaintive sound will be sustained longer than the thrum of traffic, longer than the city's pulse. The kid seems oddly familiar, maybe an extra from the movie *Brazil*?

Boohoo, you deprived member of the privileged class, there are economic theories that can explain your quest, Jonas hears himself think, *but they haven't come into focus yet, through all the ash and dust. Yes, there are blind rules of aesthetics bound to a political ideology which to transgress means not death, just this, your oblivion and obscurity.*

Jonas knows that rents in San Francisco are expensive, that rents in Toronto are expensive, that rents in London are expensive, that rents in Seattle are expensive, that rents in

New York are expensive, that rents in Paris are expensive, that rents in Iqaluit are expensive, that rents in Luanda are expensive, that rents in Tokyo are expensive, that rents in Geneva are expensive, that rents in Moscow are expensive, and that rents in N'Djamena are expensive, too.

He deduces: *All citizens are anonymous. All passers-by are citizens. Therefore, no one knows who they are, or where it is they are trying to go. Therefore no one can afford to be here. Therefore only the rich have souls —*

There is no friend, only this dream of waiting continually disturbed by a desire to flee. To move to Detroit, or Abu Dhabi!

He doesn't need methadone, though he drank some once in the mid-nineties, just for kicks, and it did nothing other than taste of Kool-Aid and bug spray and make him puke over the bouncer's eel-skin boots. The mid-nineties, Jonas recalls, was after the Berlin Wall collapsed, before the 9/11 attacks, back when drum and bass replaced jungle breaks but the club kids still knew how to party, *around the world, around the world*...

He isn't in Berlin, or San Francisco, or Toronto. He is in a mentally projected image of a place that is all borders and no exists — out of sight, out of time.

He isn't broke, but he's unemployed. He isn't homeless, but he can't pay the landlord in art or sophistry or sad stories about the disappearance of his childhood pet. He isn't old. He isn't sick. He hasn't completely lost his mind, yet.

And he isn't altogether without hope. There's always the Nobel Dropping Out of Art School Dressing Like a Clown Sitting Around Drinking Coffee All Day Bumming Cigarettes and Complaining About the Government Prize — which he's for sure in the running for.

Who says it doesn't matter or mean something to have perfected a dying art? *Give me moribund, or give me death!* Jonas battle-cries in his head.

When he was young, he could leave his body while asleep, rolling out of it slowly, then rising in the air, light as a dandelion seed. He'd drift around his bedroom, but when he tried to leave through the window his head would always bump against the glass — which woke him up.

Who says it doesn't matter or mean something to have practised the art of lucid dreaming?

It is raining. The rain freezes. Runnels of pebbly ice form in the gutters and eventually turn to slushy streams and clog up the sewer grates. And Jonas and the master of the multicoloured tubes witness this same succession of weather events — separately, unmoved, wherever the hell they are — both uninvited guests.

For just a moment, between passing cars, they meet each other's eyes, exchange stagy glances, and nod. Then Jonas wanders off, happy in the knowledge that he is wasting his life.

Lab Notes

Believing that he has willingly assumed the identity of a broken mirror shard, Subject X is now able not only to dissociate, but to reflect certain forms of psychological abuse and, at the behest of those whom he regards as his subculture's heroes (secretly our own Superintendents), he appears ready to cut out the tongues of those other subjects who too often claim that everything is "all good."

All You Get

Ignore the child chanting in your head: *gimme, gimme…*

You need an unlimited supply of little blue pills, and a unicorn wrist tattoo. You want a gas stove that looks like a woodstove, and a white-legged cat named Spooky Pants. You need a never-ending Metro Card, and an espresso machine that glitters and gleams in anticipation of a 1920s hallucination of a utopian metropolis!

Scratch & Win! Bingo! Lotto 6/49!

Want, need, what's the difference? Take all you can get, or deprive yourself. Wake up sad, eat the Sun God's cattle, go back to sleep. Get thirsty. Yo! Shut off the tap! Quit your over-the-counter medication habit, then take up pornographic acts of self-abuse.

Dalliances, ya! To hell with the truth. Feed fables to your ravenous feelings and ignore all those whose counter-arguments boast facts.

Hedonistically indulge in lack!

It's true, the cost of personal integrity is total isolation, says the cigarette to your lips. Catch me as I trip the light fantastic, says a grandiose silence to the walls. Chase me across the American Plains, to the discount mall, and I'll meet you there beneath the chandelier of plastic tears.

You see rumpled fabric: it's a Renaissance painting! You hear a siren: it's a cop show! Your mind is not your own.

Thanks to increased public surveillance, you can go anywhere — though anywhere seems to be everywhere now. And thanks to post-industrial capitalist innovation — the snozberries taste like snozberries!

Tonight you'll wear your "NEW YORK DOESN'T LOVE YOU" t-shirt to the Royal Canadian Legion and get into a scuffle. Tomorrow you'll apply for multiple citizenships, and any job that doesn't involve waffle-making anger-fits.

Network executives get drunk and fall in love every day, you think, before doubting yourself, redoubling your focus and, hunched over the blue-frozen screen, revising your five-mile home-shopping stare.

If you get rich, you'll start talking to yourself again, and maybe you'll listen. You'll phone your parents to offer condolences, even though they're both dead. You'll travel the world but end up destitute — your head full of blurred faces, crazy subway maps, and floor plans of a certain cloister museum repurposed as a third-rate casino.

Meanwhile, there goes your piggy bank, spilled from the clouds — raindrops in the Pacific!

Meanwhile, there are all these people to ignore or avoid, and the film about your life as a metaphor for a one-night stand with the breeze is about to start over, and this time you don't want to miss the opening credits!

More Bad News

Outside it is Tuesday.

Like usual, across the bay, all but the shoulder blades of the Golden Gate Bridge are lost inside a musculature of fog.

Somewhere out there are old and new friends, just waiting to be found.

Is this what they call the Tuesday Blues?

Easy, steady on. High up in the Oakland Hills, having finagled a job as a house-sitter, Jonas is an inhabitant of a stranger's life either temporarily on hold or coming to an end: Frederick G. Tuckerman, ex-husband of Jonas's chamomile tea-drinking aunt, Gemma, ex-film producer, famous raconteur, and close friend of California's governor, Jerry Brown, is sick in the hospital with wet brain and liver disease.

Still, lucky Frederick is filthy rich!

O to be cursèd, but romanticized, too.

The back terrace extends above a rolling emerald lawn that ends precipitously at a Japanese gazebo framed by a sweeping view of the whole of the bay. Back inside, there is a kitchen with a heated limestone floor and a built-in espresso maker; a library with books about crystals, American folklore, and the history of moving images; a screening room; a workout room; and a room featuring a huge mahogany bar with Art Deco glass cabinets and mirrored panels and stocked to the hilt with antediluvian whiskies and port wines! — a room Jonas refuses to allow himself to re-enter.

And everywhere, both inside and out, there are pissing cherub fountains, their streams passing through a fluctuating continuum of incandescent hues adjustable via a digital touch-screen podium, which Jonas dares not touch.

It is extremely unsettling, walking through room after room not his, sleeping covered in someone else's velvety sheets — maybe even dreaming dreams not his own?

But normalcy and routine, thinks Jonas, should provide some long-absent and much-needed sense of stability. Make the bed. Brush the teeth. Wave to the gardener, whatshisname! Sort and take out the recycling once a week. Order groceries online. Keep up a schedule of sit-ups. Shadow boxing in the screening room at night relieves stress, and makes him feel enormous! Tomorrow, he must remember to collect all the newspapers the newspaper boy always fails to throw over the redwood screening fence.

At sunrise, reading the news, even if it is from a world so far away, he lets the news creep into him, become him, his fingers stained with the authenticity of *actual* ink.

His father read the *Times*. Now here Jonas is, reading the *Times*, the *SF Examiner*, and the *Chronicle*, too. Apparently there are *Bedbugs, North Koreans, Copycat Killers, Uninvited Royal Wedding Protesters, Leaky Oil Reserves, Terror Parades, Codfish Disputes*... Apparently the hopes and dreams of the West are *Fiscally Melting, Evaporating, and Pouring Out Into Cliffs of Volcanic Steam and Ash Above Iceland's Whatchamacallit Glacier*... To top it all off, Obama was caught smoking again.

His father ate oatmeal, and now Jonas eats oatmeal, and half an organic grapefruit. No more bananas. He's cured! He feels comfort in this daily practice of eating a high fibre breakfast while reading the news. How agreeable this is, integrating with a well-informed citizenry, participating through the passive absorption of nutrition and facts.

In local news, it appears that suicides from the bridge are on the rise. The economic downturn, some experts say, could be a factor. Jonas notes the weather reports call for more rain, so he'll be sure to carry an umbrella, if he finally goes out today.

After his morning shave, Jonas tries bunching his brow into the image of a front-page headline. His eyes, he sees, are bracketed by cryptic ideograms and rest upon dark chalices. He should get out soon, break the surface, find some sort of snorkel to the *actual* universe.

Tomorrow is Wednesday, so perhaps he'll pick up a lottery ticket this afternoon. He'll be filthy rich, too! But wait, he's thinking of Lotto 6/49, and Canada, again. How can he forget? *California über alles!*

No, Jonas will never beat the system. His talents, he now sees, can only be extended by means of already well-established metaphors and tropes. Fuck his Canadian citizenship. He must flow with the power, adapt, assimilate, win the world over with a glib smile. He is already getting used to the feeling of being pleased with himself for no reason, and to the soothing sensation of this warm kitchen floor on the bare soles of his feet.

Where did all these grapefruit husks come from? He can't stop hiccupping! The morning is slipping away into nothingness. Time's a jerk…

So he calls a Yellow Cab and allows himself to be ferried along streets made of congealed fog and dropped off on Solano Avenue where, at the incongruously named Sunshine Café, he tries speaking with the Voice of an official spokesman who must acquit himself of any knowledge or guilt: "Large Americano please, half the water. Thanks!" His grin, stuck on caps lock.

But the barista, a redheaded girl with freckles and an enormous silver bull's ring dangling from her nose, avoids his gaze. Jonas goes on, "Looks like another presidential bid is about to go down with the cruise ship." Rapidly shifting his weight from foot to foot, Jonas imagines he is a boxer warming up. "But pow! That's where all this horse trading on the convention floor will getcha."

"Here or to go?" asks the barista.

"If the news were more honest, instead of a newscaster, there would be a chorus of executives!" he says.

"Sir? Will that be for here or to go?"

"Say, do you have a copy of today's *New York Times*? All this exploitation, and these death tolls, you know, and our government being run by a bunch of mass m-m-murdering c-c-capitalists!"

The barista looks at him now and tap-tap-taps angrily at her bull's ring with the silver stud embedded at the tip of her tongue. The sound grows louder and louder until it's as if someone is knocking then pounding on a steel door. Startled, Jonas tries to locate himself in the present, to move things along. But he is stuck in a sequence. He is riding a neurological ripple effect akin to how the eye falls in love with the rolling green lawns of the Berkeley Hills.

Jonas continues to speak, but without opening his mouth: *Did you know that in Canada there are signs that say: Warning To Tourists: Do Not Laugh At The Natives?*

Winking, he does a little jig, jumping and bumping his heels together, before adding, "To go, please. Thanks!"

The condiments table is a mess of cream puddles and spilled sugar crumbs. Jonas scowls then mumble-whispers into his coat sleeve: *I know she must work within a Byzantine system with limited resources, but perhaps she could learn how to delegate and to be more forthcoming about her impeding mood-quakes.*

But onwards! Tallyho! There is progress to be made. There are worlds within worlds, words within words, woes within woes. No doubt there are signs in China's factory towns that read: *Dear Valued Employees: When In Public Please*

Keep Your Mutilated Wrist Stumps Inside Your Pockets! Yes, there are countless bits of information that need to be processed, interrogated, vindicated, or simply ignored.

So. Marching through the door, the brown loafers he is wearing — borrowed from Frederick's walk-in closet and polished earlier that morning with spit — sparkling in the returned sun. So. Marching east along a newly paved sidewalk, consciously avoiding each crack. So. Marching across the street, careful to look out not only for cars but bicycle traffic. So. Jonas notices the bridge balanced above the water, a burning icon reborn among a few remaining scraps of mist — then starts to consider if the stranger following behind him crying, "Sir, hey, sir, hey you forgot your coffee, your umbrella!" has something to do with what's wrong with somebody else, or everything to do with what's wrong with him.

Hailing a cab, Jonas hurriedly settles into the back seat, thinking that later this evening he'll ensconce himself in the gazebo, with perhaps just a thimbleful of that 1963 tawny port, and watch cherubs piss rainbows at the sun as it spills into the ocean. But when the driver asks for the address Jonas can't speak, having forgotten where he lives, and whoever it is he is supposed to be.

Lab Notes

Although we have illustrated, if not scientifically then at least metaphorically, the interrelated and unified nature of the forces that comprise both Subject X's spiritual laziness and his sexual drive, so far no single theory has been able to successfully express these relationships without employing terms derived from the Internet.

Cab Ride

Jonas has a dream where, instead of telling a whole story with in-depth scenes, and rather than adhering to Newton's Third Law of action and consequence, he offers up anecdotes to his cab driver, whose phony "California Taxi" permit mounted on the dash beside a Christ figurine not so much welcoming sinners as shrugging its arms identifies the cabbie simply as "Bob." The cab smells of cinnamon and old mops, and the passenger seat resembles an open drawer spilling over with shirts and sweaters and pinstriped trousers all unevenly folded and stacked. Jonas is sitting in the back, piecing together fabulist fragments. He summarizes the latest news from the EU and relates it to one of his grandmother's old Scottish sayings, *many a mickle makes a muckle* — whatever *that* means. Weather conditions and forecasts become vague analogies for the vagaries of the human spirit.

From the cab's radio — which Jonas realizes isn't a dispatch system but a police scanner — a voice emits harsh monosyllables. "That sounds just like Don Cherry," says Jonas, wanting to explain, though he doesn't, why the way everyone hates the Toronto Maple Leafs reminds him of his Uncle Duke, who had a thrilling past but is now in the most pathetic of circumstances.

And look at all the construction in the Mission District. Nothing's the same as it was. Where's Clarion Alley? Is that a Whole Foods? These towering cranes must be sentinels sent back from the thirty-first century! And isn't it strange how every small business that burns down in the night is replaced the very next day by a glassy condominium? Who debates these rezoning policies? Where were the city plans for public review? Probably displayed in some buried location, hours past midnight, and voted on by a cabal of real-estate moguls and landscape architects in love with Ayn Rand.

The cab driver grins and shakes his head as if to say *yes*, as if to say *no*.

Jonas is on a solo, Holden Caulfield-type mission — as a kind of challenge to himself — heading off with a head full of white powders to party with a bunch of phonies on the edge of an industrial part of Oakland. Jonas re-reads the name of the event on the flyer, "Cleopatra's Asp," and imagines a space where musicians and artists have transformed their studios into work-play suites, complete with visible plumbing, tire swings, wall-sized mirrors, laser and DJ equipment, and bookshelves full of Baudrillard and Žižek.

It's been years since he snorted cocaine.

The taxi driver cruises. At first his driving style is fast and rhythmic. He snakes around pedestrians, clocks to the millisecond the duration of yellow lights, and chats amicably. "I am from Brazil," he tells Jonas, "from São Paulo, a city where music is an acute awareness of timing, my friend." Then, without warning, and with no cause or reason that Jonas can perceive, Bob slams on the brakes. His haphazard stack of clothing tumbles to the foot of the passenger seat. "Can't beat the system. Go-go with the flow!" he sing-songs.

Jonas has been a resident of Earth long enough to know that half-hidden beneath all banter with cab drivers are universal laments. Biting his nails he interrogates the quality of his tellurian existence. "I am from right here," Jonas says, feeling slightly stickmannish. "I grew up on this next block. See that Japanese maple? As a kid, I remember watching the last moon landing from up in that tree. In Technicolor, in 3-D!"

Then they cross an impossible bridge...

Bob the cabbie smiles into his rear-view mirror and says, "When I was a boy, my father was trained by a team of ex-Israeli secret service agents to be a bodyguard for a famous financier." Chirruping his horn, he makes a sharp left turn, threading through a disorientated group of lost tourists. He goes on, "But my father died in a fire he set himself. He had planned to stage a rescue, to save his employer and make himself important, a big hero!"

"I never knew my dad," Jonas replies, stoically, "but I'm related to Steve Jobs, who taught me that I can have everything I want, but nothing I actually love, or need to survive."

They drive on, Jonas and Bob, both quiet for a while. Having crossed over the water they now move through darker and darker streets, until Jonas says, "Drop me off right there please, in front of the window with the red strobe light."

Jonas deliberately over-tips. "Graças, fátuo!" says Bob, laying his new bills face-up inside a small coffin-like lockbox, his face dim, medieval, saintly, detached. Securing the lid, he tucks his box beneath his seat. "Be careful tonight, my friend," he says. "You must be safe in this part of town."

Jonas looks around the poorly lit street — nearly every entrance chained, every window boarded-up, every fence topped with razor-wire, every brick facade crumbling — and wants to ask *what good are these cities we've built if they maim and discard their own residents?* but then gets distracted searching his seat for lost coins or keys — any fragments, of himself or others, left behind.

Squinting, the cabbie from São Paulo glances towards the window pulsing in pyrotechnic display where a great thumping can now be heard, along with ear-splitting auto-tuned lyrics, "We stay up all niiiight! We get down all niiiight!" Then he adds, "And be careful of drugs. I hear there is a kind of ecstasy pill in America today so powerful and pure it paralyzes the body and freezes the mind."

"But O to be a teenager in love!" Jonas exclaims, stepping out from the cab, popping a breath mint, then checking his pockets for his invite, which is suddenly missing, and telling himself to forget it, never mind, just walk, just walk, just walk — towards the flashing red lights.

Forgetting

You still don't know where you are, or who it is you're supposed to be. You've begun to suspect that closeness is a terrible thing, all this clutching, grasping, and grappling. Whether cramped into a shopping mall, a chat room, or this underground *community*, everyone is so unyielding and so lonely that it is necessary to take shelter inside the Russian space capsule of your soul, to hide from all these insufferable tentacles and feelers.

High up, oxygenless, you look down at a slow creek spilling out and sifting through the beach rubble — bone-white shell fragments, Styrofoam, bits of broken glass polished bright as eyes — and trickling into a sea of mercury and pharmaceuticals.

But you can't be trusted. Your perception has been infected by a parasite capable of manipulating your values and beliefs. Do you actually think that your life is a rickety caboose being pulled through endless tunnels? Are you in love with these lightning-hot sparks as they burn through your skull and set fire to your memories?

Or perhaps it is all this chronic self-doubt that has made you so wildly unpredictable. Maybe fitful employment has turned your extremities green. If a mushroom containing digital spores sprouts from the top your head, you'll know for sure the cause and nature of your suffering.

"Hey, are you okay?" asks a hazy globule where a face should be — if a gargantuan dung beetle in a flesh suit should have a face.

None of this surprises you. Nothing's out of place. As a professional spectator, you've seen it all before — the ten-inch-platform-shoed transvestites, the boa constrictor fetishists, the furry yellow chicken people.

You search for an appropriate response and manage, "I guess I could use some air."

No, what's truly strange are the transmissions bouncing off satellites and careening through the stratosphere just to rattle this small speaker pressed against your ear — a little bird cheeping, "I thought you should know, I miscarried the day you left town."

Why have you come here, outside, alone? The night is cold and full of the terror of the meaninglessness of nothing but shadows and nowhere to go. There is a phone in your hand but it's dead.

Yes, you suppose it is increasingly apparent that you are impervious, that your refusal to sustain meaningful connections is the one and only constant you are willing to hold onto.

For example, whatever happened to whatshername? Patroness of the broken glass and gashed wrist? Never mind. Forget.

Put out of your mind Ursula's eyes glittered in blue —

For example, even as you try to explain to the gathering crowd about why you have just smashed a cinder block through a red flashing window, you know you sound delusional to everyone but yourself.

Maybe it was the chainsawing dubstep that triggered your vertigo, your aggression. Or was it the velvet wallpaper that fucked your head — all those cancan girls dancing in endless rows? Perhaps your failure to be recognized as a sensitive creature finally crossed wires with and short-circuited your holographic joie de vivre.

Nevertheless, now is the time when the poets must gossip to instantiate themselves. As it was in ancient Rome, so here public servants dressed all in blue stand idly by, fake-coughing into their sleeves. It seems hats with big bows are in fashion with women again. It seems their boyfriends all wear the same crazed TV sportscaster smile, that last defence against caring.

How you feel just like your childhood pet cockatoo, Webster, who escaped and who no doubt tried to speak his bits of obscene English to all the wild birds of the Pacific Northwest.

You wish Oliver were here, or Bob, or the man they call Reveen. How you want to dissolve — where silence continues, even in this social setting, to hold its constant vigil — into the background of these silhouettes.

But whether you are a clown or a sociopath, or you are simply surrounded by walking and talking pillars of nothingness, the upshot is the same.

Big Bird is here, but with the head of a man, and he is simultaneously threatening your life and trying to explain how few will appreciate the effort it takes to make threats at such a peaceful gathering.

But you know what to do. Closing your eyes you roll with the pitchpoling ship. Tomorrow, you'll burn your books on etiquette. As a cure for fever, you'll shut up a spider in the shell of a nut. To cleanse the soul, you'll swallow powdered limestone mixed with mud. You'll take all that's fragile and precious and have it hermetically entombed. Never demur to your enemies or complain to your friends. Just follow the script, and extend the logic of your position.

You've arrived in San Francisco. Oh, what fun! Maybe tomorrow you'll jump from the Golden Gate Bridge.

The Good Life

Everywhere he goes, Jonas visits the same long-lost friends. Now all of them have babies.

They have pink-headed babies with slobbery jowls. They have toothless, sponge-cake-faced babies with sea anemones for hands. Babies are strapped into jolly jumpers, towered in high chairs, stationed at rocketship control centres. Pop-star babies, clown-cheeked babies, and mastermind babies snuffling and ferreting under the blanket for a leaky nipple. There are babies popping up like corks in all the rivers and oceans. There are mushroom babies sprouting from the sodden soil. Aliens, invaders of planet Earth, this pox of babies, this plague of fecundity, star-seeds falling from the night sky!

Jonas smiles weakly. He is weak in the knees. He is weak in the stomach. He is weak in forethought and in hindsight. He has a weakness for single-malt whiskies, and for sexy flight attendants who check in on a timely basis.

Fat and sleepy-eyed, his friends invite him to sit, relax. Doffing autumnal scarves, they say they have just strolled back from the craft fair where they bought books on the art of edible origami and local art history. Now they litter their monologues with the famous last words of wildlife painters: "Every work, she is reputed to have said, was a *reproach*."

They have a miniature schnauzer and a collection of rare vinyl no one is allowed to touch. They possess lemon zesters, garage door openers, and a vast knowledge of the vicissitudes of the NASDAQ.

They wear the translucent skin of the well fed and spiritually indifferent.

Jonas has bad breath. He is bad with small talk and the botched fledgling of his polite laughter tumbles from its branch. He'll never admit to his sour habit of gritting his teeth whenever he thinks he hears someone speaking his name with a forced lack of derision. He fumbles the joke of his employment history and misses every Triple Word Score.

"So, are you seeing anyone?" they are always so gracious to ask.

"Yes," replies Jonas, "Tara and I have been together for a while now. Oh, I mean Ursula. But, um, anyway, we broke up."

How can he explain? There are years of his life he can't even think about, let alone discuss, while his alibis have become so multiple and varied to have entangled him, he imagines, in sticky strands of spider spit. Guilt is a trap his past has invented and set as a means of revenge, and not a suitable item for a genteel chat. Jonas thinks it is better to bring up anything else, maybe the issue of Beethoven's possible Moorish roots, but not remembering any pertinent details of proof, he quietly helps himself to more crackers.

But his friends are kind. When he sneezes and farts, their eyes sparkle and flicker like the edges of a 1980s television screen. Not surprisingly, his cover-up coughing fit stretches the limits of the space-time continuum.

Dinner is served and comes with more than one bottle of Barossa Valley shiraz, wherein, his hosts happily inform him, are hints of *fantastic farmhouse noises, Madagascar spies, Chicago cherries, licorice-breath, dryads, nerds, and Vanilla Ice undertones.* Indeed, Jonas is becoming acutely aware of the liquid's enormous complexity, delivered through the throat and nose and into the mind with a *Claude Monet "Water Lilies" of style, yet haunted by an inescapable sense of Amelia Earhart's death wish…*

"You know you're always welcome!" they attempt to say, though the baby is crying now, mimicking an air raid siren, its face a red agony. "Seriously! Anything you need!"

Trying not to teeter too much in the doorway, Jonas is neither arriving nor departing. A tightrope of a smile stretches across his face. Before him, his wine-flushed friends, the smell of new bread, a glowing hearth, a wailing newborn bundled in rosy globes of flesh. Behind him the bridge's fire-coloured towers stab through frozen mists.

Jonas is trying to balance on the edge of a precipice. He has a weak jaw, a weak disposition, a weak way of saying goodbye: "Thanks for the conversation, and the fine wine. Great to see you two again. And hey — congrats on the rug rat!"

Lab Notes

It has been leaked that on August 2, 2019, the Overseers will order this very Committee to destroy all records of our experiments. The order, we believe, may be yet another experiment in covert orchestration where we *will become the new subjects. The nature of the leak itself is suspect, and there is much speculation as to its origin — perhaps a power beyond the Overseers, some vastly intelligent Authorial Consciousness — and whether the leak was deliberately placed into our hands.*

Jonas in Frames

You nod off, seated at a desk, the afternoon light passing through a matrix of insatiate nerves. Déjà vu, stuck in a loop, different city, same Nowhere, thus you secretly perceive the intrinsic world as legitimate.

You are not a man but a cloud whose head is topped with a perfectly fitting blue felt fedora!

Thinking of those walrus-moustached men of yesteryear — their vatic falsehoods and fungible truths — you begin but forget how to tell. For example, what about your mother whose shadow once chafed the limelight? Rising from your red leather recliner, from inside the bonfire of another self-inflicted drought, groggy, purblind, you light a rich cigar and, loudly exhaling the first drag with a sigh, envision the unravelling existential threads.

It's all just gymnastics in the sky above the chestnut tree. It's all just rumble and boom.

Do you not believe that enough information, once gathered and incorporated, might one day crystallize into omitted chapters, missing links, dangling hooks, obscured figures, clandestine forms, and coded messages from the past imperfect tense? Such is the skill of the whole mad world lapping up against the flower of a wound, where the closed scar will be a testament to the total gravitational force of all your discrete ideas and stored facts.

Sure, you can lisp in one demotic idiom — fixed, rooted, eternal, despotic — but your words, blue and trembling, are slow-fading into the image of ashen hands upon ashen sheets, and of cars swishing by on streets becoming rivers that swirl inside your head. A lonely question mark, you go drifting too, engrossed in yourself as one who tenderly prods a bruise.

Wearing your fabricated outlook like a bourgeois trope, you cross the darkly flexing spaces in between, without anything you actually need to survive. How many times can you pretend to see the cities of the world decimated by an atomic catastrophe? The specks that constitute your identity you imagine as grains in a photograph entitled "Ecclesiastical Volutes of Smoke."

If there is a purpose to any of this it must be simply to continue without a purpose, to endure the discovery that failure is the essence of your identity, the essence of your sense of direction...

Fuck It

That's it. He is sick of these taxicab rides to and from Nothing and Nowhere.

Drinking silver polish from a porcelain mug that says "I LOVE FLORIDA," Jonas gags on the words "woe betide," then shouts, "Sarsaparilla sunspots!"

A bucket hauled from an empty well — all day this clatter of chatter inside his head.

He could go for some nineties dancehall reggae right about now — this Dizzy Gillespie buzz is cool, but it's getting him down.

Suddenly the year is 1912. Somewhere Stravinsky is hammering out *The Rite of Spring*. This is also the dawning of the age of skywriting, and while Jonas's name appears *trailing clouds of glory*, Jonas himself is lost inside an antechamber where chartreuse screens divide space into small cubicles.

"Listen," he whispers to the person he once might have been, "the rumours that a genderless psychiatrist in oil-stained coveralls has confined us to the outer limits of the Ottoman Empire are not altogether unfounded."

If only I could stop thinking — he thinks — *about the sable garment industry's link to certain autoerotic techniques...*

The screens ripple and glimmer, the very essence of sea air made flesh.

According to the Voice, another hirsute leafleteer has exposed herself at a Norwegian Yacht Club in East London, and now a copse of balsam fir must be razed!

All these years later, and here is the antiseptic scent his grade three teacher still lurks behind. "Everyone knows Shakespeare was a *fake*," she says, smiling like the Himalayan mountain range seen from space.

Never mind the bridges, which some people survive. Here, little white death-moths are perched on each satellite.

"Or guardian angels," Jonas speaks aloud, staring at his knuckles as they compress to pale stones. "Or you, Voodoo Stick Pins, though I loved your half-sister, Tara, Queen of the Yukon, more."

Tonight, the cosmos is a Hammond organ coughing up crucifix nails. Tonight, his poem is a river of rusted machines. And beneath: all these incessant whirs, clacks, and squeaks — noisy signifiers of his so-called existence?

He has lost Mr. Sock, and so now has nothing to live for.

He is a whiz kid of words, and his final felicitous phrase will be "fuck it."

"Up there is blue skies!" sings Dizzy, dizzily, "Down there is the sea! Over here is a great big whale, and he's looking at me!"

The Ferry to the Kingdom of the Afterlife

How did he get here? How many days and nights — *il ne faut pas dormir, mon fils, ne pas dormir* — has he been travelling? And what is this thing, so round, so sweet? There is a nice jammy spot at the centre he licks. It is the strawberry heart of a cookie he eats — finally, a treat at the centre of this labyrinth!

Jonas has been carried by cable cars, busses, airplanes, and what he imagines must be some kind of terrible fate. Now he is leaning over the deck of the Queen of Dystopia and staring into the Georgia Strait where he has just tossed his cellphone, expired driver's licence, passport, and credit cards, on this, his final trip to Who Knows Where via Who The Fuck Cares.

Just as he suspected, his credit cards don't float.

To stop shaking, he smokes half a cigarette. Smooth energies stroke the length of his limbs, flare, then gutter at the cooling tips of his extremities. Like the cookie, this too is good. This is grand, sweet, a life more than tinged with excess.

And even though it rains, and the sky is the colour of the eyes of Sisyphus — and even though Jonas has no idea how all this weather and water ever arrived here on planet Earth — he feels he somehow belongs, *merrily merrily...*

Regardless of the womb that conceived him, or the digital matrix that lulled and deceived him or, back at the beginning, the multifarious shapes and shades his soul became once it sprung from the first amino acid chains concocted in the primordial scum just to fuck him up and confuse him — he feels he belongs, whether or not it has all been a dream.

(In the Kingdom of the Afterlife, nothing's ironic.)

He belongs — not to a city, or a lifestyle, or a language, or a theory of genetics, or a figment of late-capitalism. He belongs to himself now, and thanks to the secrets of necromancy, he can do whatever and go wherever he goddamn wants —

O hubris! O endless series of cracked reflections!

Here, in this place, once and for all, poetry is dead.

Which is fine, because he wants to scour and cleanse his intelligence of all art and politics. He is so sick of his tribe that he plans to quit Facebook, maybe this time for good! He intends to cash in all of his valuable coins and rare stamps and first editions. He'll withdraw the last of his money and send the sum of his bills spinning and spiralling over the edge of the Capilano Suspension Bridge.

The night before, he vaguely remembers, he shaved his three-day beard, his head, his eyebrows, and his chest. Now when he moves his arms or his shoulders his undershirt snags on the stubble tips, sending electric pangs and thrills along the cut nerves — O what small bleeding stumps of feeling!

"Who knows what Jonas is thinking," thinks Jonas aloud, realizing that he is muttering of himself in the third person.

Three gulls glide along, drafting the ferry's broad slipstream — one gull surging into the future near the bow, one hanging abreast the bulwark Jonas leans against, and one trailing on an invisible string above the ferry's retreating wake.

Instead of wooing an audience or counting his blessings or tediously assembling another elaborate conceit, Jonas needs another cookie, another *hey-ladies-come-hither* roll of the dice! If he is going to survive, he must indulge in every sweet thing on this ship.

The alternative is also tempting. The vistas beyond — the folds of mist obscuring the treed coastline, and the more rarefied mists streaming like blue smoke from the hills — all seem beautiful, and deadly. Jonas feels Mercer's presence and shivers for the last time.

But let's stay on board, he thinks. The fact of this steel vessel floating along is sweet — yet the ship itself is no great mystery. What's impossible is that there's something beneath it all — these pulsing green waters, these many fingers of jade — that which enables him to exist, to continue — *this* is what truly terrifies, and delights!

The wind is cold. The rain still wants to discourage all living things with its tiny bloodless caresses. Jonas thinks to say a little prayer then thinks better. He thinks about having another cigarette but decides instead to go back in.

Only the last gull remains, still in tow like a nagging afterthought, its companions having headed for shore.

Lab Notes

Notwithstanding our institutional paranoia, our new results appear to demonstrate the ductility and malleability of the subject (though who the subject is *exactly, is now questionable) when force-fed a justifying ideology and provided a Canada Council arts grant. In the end we hope our experiments have illustrated, above all, the impossibility of our research ever coming to an end.*

Back on Land

What? Either someone is hammering out there, relentlessly hammering the horizon, nailing the four corners of this circus tent down — or there is a knock at the door.

You have awoken, a clown from hell. In the mirror you see your lips and mouth smeared an abysmal coal-black from whatever it was the doctors forced you to swallow.

Look at your trembling hands — puppets in the nude? No, these are the hands of an attempted murderer.

Look at your feet — terrestrial devotees? No, these are the feet of the one who tried to walk you right off the planet.

Your head is full of scraping-the-bottom-of-the-oven sounds. Where's the red violin your mother once played on the piers of the Vieux-Port de Montréal? Or the Aeolian harp you once heard inside the pink canyon walls of Sedona? Where's the jazz-flute solo you were promised if you vaulted this spangled Pleasure Dome?

Whoops. A crow just farted then hopped over a crocus. A dwarf drank a beer and belched. No one noticed. Who cares.

So what if another Save The Old-Growth Rain Forest calendar gets shredded and your days and months turn not to New Year's confetti but to colourless fodder?

The next time you dream of sailing away, you'll stay fast asleep.

The next time the world ends, you'll let all the well-meaning counsellors, dieticians, barroom mystics, junkie slum landlords, culture-game-playing artists, and each and every baby boomer left for dead who refuses to die — you'll let them all coalesce into the white noise of interstellar static the Big Bang left behind.

But it's all beginning again...

Cue the acrobats! Cue the furry yellow chicken people! Cue the dancing bears!

These Happy Carefree Days

Jonas's days are unfocused and rife with ellipses. He has starved all winter — a flâneur, surviving on the free sandwiches and coffee they serve at AA meetings and luncheon dates with ex-girlfriends — but there is still more winter to come. He is retracing his steps — passing through various moods and remembrances of his old hometown, the City of Gardens — and subject only to those laws that govern the trajectories of clouds.

His wanderings end when he is ordered to attend a job-finding workshop where, seated at a conference table with a group of newly released ex-convicts, Jonas is asked by a young woman in a powder-blue pantsuit to consider how martial artists chop several boards at once. Apparently these experts can get things done. They know how to focus their attention *beyond* the wood, on the spot where they want their flying fists to arrive. "Concentrate," Jonas is instructed, "not on the obstacles along the way, but on your ultimate career goal!"

A new Voice sings inside Jonas's head: *Kiaiii! The world you desire can be won. It exists. It is real. It is possible. It is yours. Charge!* Part of him worries about who he has been, another about who he is becoming.

On Government Street he tries not to envy every healthy and prosperous human being whose eyes he meets, telling him with the same look that no one will ever love him.

Life isn't fair, the old Voice intrudes, and Jonas is in total agreement.

But he is learning to subsume his desires with prayer: *God, grant me the serenity...* and to make gratitude lists, giving special thanks to Social Services for his single room above a Szechuan restaurant and his view of a brick wall spray-painted with a giant red "A" bursting out of its circular frame.

Then Tara calls out of nowhere and asks why it is that every man she becomes involved with is a liar and a piss-tank cheat. "It's not them, it's you!" Jonas declares. He has been reading a lot of books about self-esteem. He explains that hurt people hurt people, and how everyone he knows is a glutton for abuse, whether self-inflicted or otherwise. He asks Tara if she wants to go for lunch.

She responds, "I live in Whitehorse, you crazy fool."

"So what? Get on a plane! Steal a canoe! Just follow the sound of my voice. Are you there still? Hello?"

At dusk, smoking cigarettes outside the church, sober drunks form in a row beneath a dripping awning, shifting and bumping one another, gentle as a row of doves. Jonas stands apart, more comfortable smoking inside the soon-to-be black-rain night. He stands perfectly still, just watching the moving mouths of the others and trying to imagine their words are kind and wise.

Early the next morning Jonas can't sleep. He needs to assess the years gone by. Most of his time on Earth, he realizes, has been taken up with running around trying to stop things from going up in smoke. His past is scattered with extinguished fires, and some still smoulder underground. The only secrets he's ever kept have been his own.

Looking out his window he sees the red anarchy symbol — now slightly aglow in a weak wash of sun — as suddenly ominous. He shuts the blinds, drifts off awhile, then wakes too soon, famished and light-headed. The dawn is intruding, unhurried but inexorable, filtering through in radiant bars that fall misshapen across his rumpled sheets. It's a soft cage he's in, the confines of his life.

But no, strike that. He's a prisoner of hope! One day he'll have a job and a love affair to keep himself afloat. In the shower he sings, "Such happy carefree days are these!"

(Naturally, in dreams, you think you're wide awake.)

Wanting to call Tara back, Jonas drops the soap and runs dripping to the hallway phone. O cursèd antiquated landline! If only he could find or remember her number he might apologize, or confess, or accuse her of hypocrisy. But no, he's confusing her with Ursula, he realizes, before crawling back into bed, soaking wet.

Once again, Jonas stands in the rain outside the church. He lights a cigarette but holds onto the match, transfixed. He knows the flame loves to burn, that it was born with a necessary yearning, heat both its essence and appetite. It creeps, a blind love, feeling its way through the dark toward his fingertips. That delicate part of him waits — each cell resolute, dumbly steeled in the tight attitude of imminent pain — waits for flame to challenge flesh, that sudden graceless sensation when the will confronts desire.

Smack

Then Jonas gets one last chance.

A non-profit society, run by a twitchy salt-and-pepper-haired gentleman known to have been spun through more recovery houses and treatment centres than anyone else still living, hires Jonas to work in its Downtown Eastside office.

Nothing about this makes sense. Jonas can't even remember having applied, so he simply imagines himself falling through each moment like a soldier stumbling towards the faceless enemy across the no man's land at the Battle of the Somme.

The job demands yet another long-distance move, a new pair of shoes, no running with scissors, much false cheer, and the flattening of his senses into spreadsheets and technical gobbledygook.

He learns what it means to collate. He joins ranks with his complaining co-workers who describe each new problem as a "logistical nightmare."

Somewhere are the deprived ones whose lives this non-profit is allegedly devoted to saving, but Jonas rarely sees them *inside* the office. He only deals with paperwork, updating the intake information of new clients and filing monthly reports with the Ministry. Funding must be maintained, the system buttressed. Everything depends upon the shoring up of numbers with other numbers.

Meanwhile, the grey and white patterns of wind-broken clouds appear in Jonas's cubicle window and shift the gears of his attention. He is lucky to have a window. He keeps it open for a breeze of sanity, but still the hands of the wall clock become wavy tentacles, and he can't focus for more than a few minutes as his vision segments into disjointed frames whenever he swivels his head.

It is bad enough that during the day he is plagued by hallucinatory tintinnabulations, but then at night these tinny chimes overwhelm his consciousness, killing all hope of sleep. His waking dreams are of seeing his mouth in the mirror with his lips and teeth all photocopier-toner black.

Other times he sees himself drinking coffee with Frank and something always goes wrong, some absurdly violent incident occurs just as Jonas jolts with a start to wonder if he has actually been sleeping or just drifting off—

He counts the minutes until dawn, craving a slip back into oblivion, which never comes.

At work he counts the minutes until lunch, then later, he counts the minutes until the day's end. It is Friday night, but then it is Monday morning again, the rubber soles of his Hush Puppies squeaking and echoing along the corridor, making him flinch, as begins yet another torturous countdown to the world of partitions, counterfeit light, obligatory smiles, small talk, and unnatural units of time.

Within the confines of the workweek, inside these rooms of documents, it's as if the whole spectrum of what there is to feel and understand is compressed into greyscale.

In a feeble attempt to claim his usefulness, Jonas clicks his mouse, opening and closing the same desktop folder, over and over. And as he is struggling to smother a desire to bolt from his desk, sprint out of doors, and throw himself into the unmeasured expanse of the Pacific, something finally happens.

Floating across the room, Jonas sees a curvilinear figure in a short plaid skirt and black knee-high boots advancing towards him. She is something from a memory, a fantasy, a desire he can't fulfil. O mysterious quest object, forever out of reach! He twigs, with a twitch, that this must be the new data entry assistant, on her way, it would seem, to the cubicle adjoining his.

(But surely you must recognize her for who she is. It's Voodoo Stick Pins disguised as an office temp! Both of you are secret agents, though neither of you will ever admit it. Yes, Jonas, sometimes a good cover becomes so second nature that it takes over and your true identity withers.)

Her thighs appear to glimmer like...like fluorescent butter!

Jonas rises to greet her, but his knees start shivering, so he steadies himself against the wall with his hand, which knocks the clock, causing it to fall, bounce off his head, and drop though the open window. Amazed, he watches as it rolls across the street and slips into a sewer grate.

A crackhead ambles by doing a spasm-dance, flailing her arms and bucking her legs. Jonas waves then shakes his index finger excitedly towards the sewer grate, but the crackhead just smiles toothlessly back, shuddering along as if all this is perfectly normal and the world is well. On a nearby telephone pole a poster reads:

> *TO ALL THOSE WHO LIKE TO SHOOT HEROIN ALONE, CAREFUL! THERE'S SOME SHIT ON THE STREETS THAT'S MAKING PEOPLE DROP LIKE FLIES. DO WHAT YOU GOT TO DO TO STAY ALIVE AND NOT BREAK THE HEARTS OF THOSE WHO LOVE YOU.*

Dizzy, Jonas sits down again, somehow unnoticed or politely ignored by the new girl who is now busy setting up her desk with supplies. There, on the spot, Jonas invents a horror movie title — *To Hell With The Living Dead!* — but can't think of how to make this sound funny or smart, especially considering the tenuous nature of the lives of his theoretical clients, and the sensitive temperaments of his colleagues. Just last week his Michael Jackson "Thriller" analogy bombed at the water cooler.

Instead, Jonas asks if he can borrow her steel ruler. "Shoor," she says, blinking her twinkling blue kohl-rimmed eyes twice, grinning, then spinning one and a half times around in her office chair. Jonas sees there are two cross-angled chopsticks protruding from the blonde pinwheel at the back of her head, and he has to stop himself from asking if she ever uses them to eat sushi. "I'm Jonas," he says at last, "Jonas Ignatius Hallgrimsson the Third," and offers her a spotty banana from his desk's top drawer. She declines with a raised eyebrow and wrinkled nose.

He discovers her name is Suzanne, and they chat a bit about their respective office duties and their common dislike of Vancouver rain and rental prices. The minutes dissolve as the conversation turns to the recurring earthquake dream Suzanne has been having, which Jonas would like to interpret, if only he knew where to begin. He loves how she gestures, waving her hands through the air as she speaks, and how cautiously measured her English is with only the slightest trace of a Swedish accent. Her nails are the colour of a deep flesh wound and bedecked with tiny white dragons. Jonas won't look at her legs. He can't look. Then he does and she immediately catches his gaze. Panicked, he shuts his eyes and fake-sneezes.

"Gesundheit?" says Suzanne, wryly perplexed. Yet Jonas finds in her eyes' implied smirk a warm reassurance, as if his misbehaviour has become a kind of wonderful secret between them. Emboldened and buoyed with a sudden desire to entertain, Jonas relays in a confessional rush all the details of his own waking-dream-vision from last night...

In the dream he spells the word "HUNGRY" with bloodtipped toothpicks on a flaking Formica counter. He is in love with a girl who used to work here, who has since changed her name from Voodoo Stick Pins to Waterfall (aka Suzanne, but keep *this* secret to yourself). Frank is sitting with his back to the window, practicing his Creamo finger-flip magic, waiting on a coffee refill, and looking tense.

Having recently been insulted by a sanctimonious jazz aficionado, Frank feels like a hologram on power-save mode. He started his journey in poverty on Saint-Laurent Boulevard and hoped to end with cocaine dust and Venetian masks littering his Uptown Manhattan apartment's marble floor — not as just another visa overstayer in the Empire State.

He tells Jonas all of this telepathically while violently swivelling his head around as if he is being menaced by a mosquito.

In the dream, Jonas inhabits a number of places simultaneously and imagines himself taking on one of several possible identities: *survivor of fatal illnesses; office worker; failed artist; unicorn hunter; full-time drifter,* etc.

In the end he decides he will become a pre-adolescent riding his new BMX bike through an eternal summer vacation.

"You missed Sticks last night," says Frank, jolting Jonas back into the present.

"Missed what?"

"Duh. Remember Waterfall? Voodoo Stick Pins? I call her Sticks. She was at the cellar door. The Thursday meeting on DeKalb. Took a six-month marble."

"A marble? For six months?" Jonas asks flatly, yet secretly amazed.

"Yeah, you know, they give out marbles for clean time there. Like getting your marbles back. Look, don't take this the wrong way," says Frank, leaning in, "but you might think about showing up next time. Maybe make an amends."

Frank starts to roll a Drum cigarette on the Formica countertop, his face a portrait of absorbed detachment, the window's natural light clarifying the details of his yellow-stained fingers and dirt-caked nails. *Musician's fingers*, Jonas recalls.

The restaurant din intrudes with its chatter and clinking cutlery. On the far wall a clock's hands move backwards, the numbers all in reverse, a gimmick from a mirror universe.

"Fuck Socialism," Frank says dreamily, after he has licked the paper's yellow glue strip and rolled his smoke closed with his thumbs. "I'm trying to cultivate an absolute monarchy of the mind."

"Yeah, me too. I'm a rugged individualist," Jonas hears himself say, still staring at his toothpick sign.

Frank continues, oblivious: "The grandeur of classical music and art came from an age when authority was feared and obeyed. So now I do jumping-jacks and I jog. That's my standing army, so I can get into it if I have to. Basic defence. I do chores, like shopping and cleaning, you know, scut work and maintenance. That's the peasant part of me staying in its place. It's a well-built hierarchy, all in service to the aristocracy and royalty, by which I mean my innate nobility, the higher aspects of my nature, my thinking and feeling."

Frank's head keeps turning from side to side. He is speaking more to the invisible mosquito than he is to Jonas. Some small white things parachute from his beard onto his lap. The cook hits the order bell, loud as an alarm. "Round one! Come out fighting!" yells Jonas. A plate breaks in the kitchen and voices erupt.

The waitress is back, her pencilled-on eyebrows threatening to flee into her hairline. "This coffee tastes funny," says Frank, making a face, his unlit Drum sticking out stagily from a corner of his mouth.

"Well, mon petit," says the waitress, stretching her index finger out from the coffee pot handle to point to the spot between Frank's eyes, "that's because it was made by a *clown*," and she wiggles her eyebrows.

"If you think I'm *sexy*, and you want more *coffee*, come on baby let me *knoooooow*," Jonas offers then snorts before cupping his mouth nervously with his hands.

But Frank is no longer in the mood for coffee, and he covers his cup with his hand just as the waitress — suddenly smiling across the room at someone she recognizes — begins to pour fresh coffee from her pot.

Everything that happens next happens in a flash, then stops. Snapshot: Frank's electrified face, his dilated pupils, his outstretched arms. Only the waitress moves, slowly backing away as Frank's curses cut the air.

Jonas is laughing and can't stop. Suzanne, he notices, isn't laughing, but her blue kohl-rimmed eyes are floating curiously in space, still gazing towards him, so he carries on…

In the dream Jonas is laughing. What's the point of bearing witness to another's loss of himself, other than to lose oneself in hiccupping hysterics? (In the dream your feet are pedalling under the Formica counter. They are bicycling under the office desk as you chortle and gasp. Letting go, your handlebars trained ahead, your body a perfect momentum, your mother calling from an unfamiliar distance, from a place suddenly removed in time, the table set for dinner, and the darkening of the hour forgotten in the whizz of pavement beneath your new BMX tires…)

Rigidly upright, his shoulders aligned, his eyes squinched shut, Frank hammers both fists on the table, and repeats, "God*damn*! God*damn it*, lady!" — with his Drum cigarette somehow still dangling, stuck to his lip.

(Racing along a gravel path to the waterfall, its silver already rushing in your ears, you know the fantastically named girls have all gone on ahead. They will meet you either somewhere in the miraculous future or, if you happen to lose focus and swerve, at the corner of Nowhere and Too Late, at the Atlas Bistro where Frank, your last friend, now sits lost in his own rage.)

Jonas wonders if he should try patting Frank gently on the back. But then Jonas thinks better. (There can be no alliances.)

Suzanne's office chair is empty. Her blue kohl-rimmed eyes have flitted away. The lights are dim. It's almost six o'clock and no one's around...

The next morning Jonas marches into the office early, clean-shaven, wearing a white necktie with red polka dots, eau de cologne, and a new cloak of cheerfulness. But beneath his cloak he feels sick, a thing burdened with appetites. The office has become a maddening realm of confused possibilities.

By noon he is numb again. Suzanne has failed to materialize and Jonas wonders about his visions from yesterday morning. Or was it afternoon? Or ever?

Bent over the photocopier's jammed paper tray, feeling zombie-like and resigned to his fate, Jonas is speaking in low tones to a machine that wants nothing but to offend and to foil him — when suddenly he feels a tremendous *SMACK* across his ass!

He leaps. He catches his breath, looks around.

"Hello Jone-*azz*," says Suzanne (aka Voodoo Stick Pins, aka Waterfall), smirking, slowly blinking, then poking out the pink tip of her tongue while menacingly brandishing the steel ruler above the half-moon of her hip.

Jonas's heart rushes the stage, the Voice becoming a Crowd of Voices roaring in his ears. His buttocks tingle and sting, a sensation which spreads through his whole body while the surfaces and contours of the room blur and dissolve into an amorphous wash flooding his brain.

Just then the worried countenance of his boss pokes around the corner and chirps — "What was that sound? A gunshot? Did I miss something?"

That night Jonas sleeps like the dead. The *truly* dead. Having all he desires, his dreams are of no dreams, of silence, of nothingness.

The next day he quits.

Village Life Nostalgia

Then it snows and Jonas is transported to a village on the west coast of British Columbia, famous for its glass fishing floats, Byronic heroes, and driftwood sculptures.

He trudges from the bus stop into town, hoping to partake of the local scene, while hedging that his designation of stranger will imbue him with mystique and free him from the burden of other people's lives.

But the hostel is closed. Molly's Beach has shut its doors for renovations. The Craft Bazaar is no more.

Yesterday he was in the company of multitudes. Today, the future breeds a silence that expands into white landscapes indistinguishable from the sky, an infinitude blurring with anonymity.

Down at the docks, trawlers and crab boats bob idly like ragtag bodies waiting for the homeless shelter to open. Jonas looks out across the Salish Sea at a misty vista suggestive of a screen saver.

(In a moment of clarity you might perceive the mechanism of your own mind as it swerves away from the reality it knows is there and towards its own obsessive making and unmaking, false surmise, and sad perplexity. Why can't you simply see what *is*? Because we won't allow it — and we are the Authors of your Being.)

Fuck this, thinks Jonas, *I should go back to New York*.

A feeling constricts his chest then takes him by the wrists. Memory's strange, how it prods the places which hurt the most — the image of his father standing in the wheelhouse of his classic wooden motor yacht, squinting and gritting his teeth while threading the eddying eye of Active Pass on his way to Keats Island. Never to be seen again! This whole coast is haunted by an odyssey from some long-ago time — echoes threatening to drive Jonas mad.

His father — who once claimed to have smoked opium with Ezra Pound's widow in a confessional in the *Salute* in Venice, where he boasted to her that he was translating Dante into Swahili, just for fun…

But Jonas knows that all these stories are self-originating myths.

His father, outdoorsman, illusionist extraordinaire, ex-secret service agent who wrote an epic poem about particle physics at age six — all these subjective distortions Jonas refused to believe or endorse, until he himself became afflicted by the very same sins, and the Voice.

With one cigarette left and just enough money for a coffee, he follows a main road uphill, searching for somewhere to linger. The road is littered with dirty crusts of ice and flanked with evergreens whose lichen- and moss-covered trunks are the masts of ancient shipwrecks. Near the top of the rise, tucked away inside an enclave of fir, the Black Eye Café appears with its small patio and three snow-covered benches.

Even if everyone else in this smug nation is downing flaming shots of absinthe and dancing the fandango, Jonas, whose accomplishments have gone without praise, whose best traits have been ignored, will sit here, lost in himself, child of loneliness and mystery, and he will shiver and weep!

But later, while searching his pockets for a lighter he doesn't have, Jonas knocks his cup, its contents spilling over and staining the pages of a Victorian novel that flexes and brims with a kind of protracted syntax he has only just begun to appreciate — such as: "It seemed that this enthusiast was just as cautious, just as much alive to judgments in other minds as if he had been that antipode of all enthusiasm called 'a man of the world,'" etc.

Jonas reads with the page turned upside down, craving a different perspective. The sense is pleasurably tortuous, and the contents strike an uncanny chord — though now the coffee-infused ink is bleeding all over the page, sentences smearing into Rorschach blots, which resemble bat moths and rainclouds and fish fins and skulls and shadows of his mother's spindly hands. The book is a whirlpool Jonas stares at, a dizziness of blurred figures and symbols that threatens to pull him down, perhaps into the bowels of the beast itself.

He is shaking a bit, the only one crazy enough to be out in this weather, yet still Jonas fears that at any moment someone might sit down beside him here on this wet bench — mentor, priest, cultural elder, maybe the Old Man himself — and begin to philosophize — while stroking his seaweed beard down the length of his neck and glinting his eyes madly towards the cold, white, overcast sky — about the war years, or the hippie revolution, or the dotcom bust, or the end still to come...

What is the Holocaust, the Old Man might say, *without me? Who remains to speak on behalf of Hiroshima's irradiated silhouettes? Only I was there. Only I saw the shit go down right before Mao Zedong was caught whispering the word "rosebud" in his sleep.* Citizen Kane, *let me tell you, wasn't directed by Orson Welles, but by Frank Sinatra, who was really Veronica Lake in drag. No, I didn't fight in Korea and Vietnam on the very same day, but I did fix the Arab–Israeli conflict inside my head while mastering my Montgomery Clift stare. It's true, Stalin orchestrated the overthrow of Elvis's management, but it was actually Jackson Pollock who planned and funded the Bay of Pigs, just like it was Fellini's* La Strada *that triggered the Troubles in North Ireland via the putative butterfly effect, though no one knew about that then. And anybody who knows anything knows that JFK wasn't the* only *President to kiss a nuclear missile on its nose-tip. You bet I had a dream, which I achieved when I piloted Apollo 11 through the first computer video game simulation of Spacewars! But when Bob Dylan's electric guitar reflected Anton LaVey's newly shaved head, this not only led to the death of French Canada, but to the kidnapping of the entire Black September terrorist organization by Margaret Thatcher's memoirist. As I had predicted, new facelift technology meant that neoliberals everywhere could emulate person-to-person relations with Pierre Trudeau. But listen carefully to what comes next. In 1978, the Sony Walkman is built by a character in Kurt Vonnegut's* Breakfast of Champions *right at the point where the narration switches to the present tense. Soon thereafter, John Lennon is replaced by the Commodore 64. Think about it! Liberace, after riding the Scream Machine at Vancouver's Expo '86 and going deaf, disappears somewhere inside Chernobyl's number four reactor! The next day, Madonna's bra appears on the outside of her shirt, Bill Gates's body is replaced by an alien pod, and it's goodbye Space Shuttle Challenger, hello sea change...*

Jonas wants to interrupt and go back to the year he was born when sideburns reappeared from the nineteenth century and the Twin Towers were the world's tallest crow's nests. He wants to torture a confession from tenderness, to rewrite his past, not as a self-consciously constructed case study, but in lines publishable as art.

But who is talking to whom?

Jonas is tired. What's the point of continuing on like this, endlessly speculating, confabulating? Perhaps he is only obsessed with the loss of each outgoing breath, and with impossible schemes to reverse the process.

It is snowing and it will continue to snow, flakes the size of cabbage moths. And even though these are the days when Jonas can barely stand his own company — when he wishes he could look into the window's glass and see only *through* — he still prefers himself to the company of strangers, or of ghosts, or of anyone he's ever known. Even if the Old Man still lives, with his ten thousand tales of albatrosses, Jonas no longer gives a shit.

Through the darkening trees he glimpses the road into town, now covered in snow like an arm inside a white fur coat. No one's coming or going. He's so cold he's warm.

Lab Notes

In summary, more than any real life situation it is the subject's ability to project itself into Philip K. Dick novels that predominantly shapes its behaviour. These findings are attuned to the thought vibrations of a long dead but legendary subject who once filed its reports with an Administer who happened to be no other than another facet of the subject's very own "artistic temperament" — who was later administered agonizing and dangerous shocks in the form of high doses of amphetamines and self-admonishments. In both cases, which were one and the same, there were bloody revolts within the cells of its body. Still, in every case thus far observed, the mutation has been contained.

Notes for a Poem (Revised as a Flashback)

At some point in the future there will be only the past — or so says the Voice of today.

Standing in queue for the hand sanitizer, you overhear the gossip and the meandering talk, so now you know the new intern's name is Phil, and how many handmade quilts have been donated for veterans (three), and of a remarkable thing that occurs in the blood when the flagging force of its pressure fails to exceed earth's downward tug —

Your desire to flee the flickering fluorescents, to escape white spidery hands sewn into white cotton sheets — a mockery of palliative care's décor printemps — and the need for a common, untortured language — this is what brings you here, to be among the swing shift staff gabbing between the Gift Shop and Nowhere.

No poetry, no art. No words, but for the sake of words, behind which you have discovered what distinguishes the doctor's superior view — his eyes all green lightning bugs, all flecks of jade embedded in quartz. He alone stands silently!

Forget your mother, her stroke-withered arm — fingers gnarled, useless — and the vase of tulips she knocks to the floor. Never mind the blood-red petals, the water, the shards. And how she keeps pleading for things you only half-understand: *Laissez-moi dormir. Pourquoi ils ne me laissent pas aller? Je veux dormir…*

Because now someone is joking that Phil is the kind of genius who writes Socrates quotes on the bathroom wall and forgets to zip up his pants. *Laughter.* Then all go quiet — interns, orderlies, nurses, and physicians alike. Everyone's hands scrubbed aseptically clean, rosy pink. The doctor's eyes, ever sparkling.

Because now you feel a fire welling up behind your solar plexus, then moving through your esophagus, and into your throat...

[*Here several pages have been lost.*]

The Heron

At first he has the idea to swim over with a cellphone wrapped in a plastic bag clenched in his teeth. But he knows the appearance of distance is the soul of deception, and he's not as strong a swimmer as he once was.

Instead, he steals a flat-bottomed wooden skiff and rows from Grantham's Landing to Keats Island, thinking: *Yo, Odysseus! I'll race you home!*

It is early January and many of the island's moss-roofed summer cabins are uninhabited. Breaking a sliding door's latch and entering is a cinch. Soon the blue and orange flames from a driftwood fire are waltzing together inside a medieval-looking hearth made of interlocking slabs of sandstone now alive with billowing sail-shaped shadows.

Sultan-like, Jonas lolls inside a nest of embroidered pillows, his feet propped before the chain-link fire screen, as he talks drunkenly on his cell. To Voodoo Stick Pins, aka Waterfall, aka Suzanne, he says, "I can't make you love me." To Frank he says, "I can't stop." To Oliver he says, "I can't think straight," and to Tara, just before the call drops, "I can't go for that."

There are others, but they are out of reach. He is so far away.

Night passes without sleep. Dawn slides from black to grey to a soft silvery white, then at daybreak Jonas goes outside, sits on a freezing log and watches the sun drill stars into the waves, and listens to the waves spill voices onto the sand.

On a railing at the far end of a decrepit dock, a Great Blue Heron hunches inside the shadow of its name. Either nothing happens at the right time, or everything happens right when nothing is supposed to occur. *But now is the time,* says the heron's gloomy appearance. *Now the story threatens to take shape.*

Jonas smokes and imagines a bank robber who retires to Las Vegas to sell fish food, and all the tears that must fall from the eyes of God.

Jonas has a dry cough, and a dry itchy scalp which requires a new super-moisturizing formula. His clothes are out of date, his phone bill is overdue, and ever since he returned from the States his fears that he has forgotten the best parts of his life have ballooned.

Later to Melville's pasty leviathan, its crinkled and protruding caveman brow. Forget the men on deck covered in unctuous fluids, slick as newborns fallen from the breach. Today, fear sparkles over the surface of everything like...electrified Saran Wrap!

But all these false starts and false descriptions make holes in the world — each syllable pulling one world after another into further darkness. What's left is not enough, just sea rhythms and the ageless predation of meanings.

What remains is a life that is lacking — and it has all been a pack of lies anyhow. He has been an unwitting soldier in a proxy war. He has been trapped in a maze and abused by powers he barely comprehends.

The heron is a beautiful and incomprehensible fact. Jonas throws a small stone at it and misses. Uncoiling its neck, the great bird launches the unlikely apparatus of itself with a slow battery of flaps, screeching out murderously as it drags its stick-like legs towards the open ocean.

Jonas knows that somewhere out there a vast province of plastic trash turns slowly, gathering into itself more of itself, a sluggish tempest.

He knows another celebrity sex tape on the loose means more than all the oceans' undiscovered mountains and valleys.

He knows there are oil tankers whose rainbow-suspender-wearing captains have undiagnosed mood disorders. At night, distress flares and rockets outnumber the stars.

In the distance the great bird has shrunk to the size of a moth. It goes trembling over the waves. Jonas stands and walks after it. He tries to swim back.

Lab Notes: Addendum

We have reorganized the laboratory only to find that the new structures have failed in ways we could never have anticipated. Now Subject X is staring right at us! Dear Colleagues, the following instructions are critical: do not turn your back, or bend down to get something to throw at it. Barking like a dog will not achieve anything constructive. Maintain eye contact at all times — but for the love of Apollo and all of his priests, attempt no more hypotheses.

Epilogue

Did you think you could remain as you were forever, with the red wine in your head, with the red wind in the canyon where you slept one night dreaming of night in another place?

It comes on its own now, slipping beneath the door at the corner of West Twelfth Street and Nowhere, the angel of better brain chemistry prophesying the cities you'll slum through next, the rooms you'll inhabit — the ones with grey windows streaked with silver ciphers of rain.

Is it rain tap-tapping at the glass?

No, it is someone typing on an old Remington without paper or ribbon.

No, it is someone playing a reedless clarinet, all anxious fingering and useless breath.

No, it is this: as stars point the way so stones mark the path among trees in flower leading to a bridge that floats above the moon's reflection shattered by a stream of Li Po's piss!

Will your neuroses ever be decoded, your synapses parsed, and everything explained?

Can Aristotle's unities be untied? Well, not quite.

Chatterton, Coleridge, Shelley, Keats Keats Keats Keats... Oh, please — make it *stop*!

The dream you are having is not a dream but an awareness of being, and having long been, asleep.

Perhaps one day you'll know *true* suffering, or at least glimpse the black regrets you didn't even know you had.

Perhaps you'll go deep into the medieval woodlands of Brooklyn and never come back. You'll clothe yourself in mud and verdant mosses. Yes, you'll spank that sexy ukulele — sick fuck!

No, instead forget. Avoid the sun in order to reclaim it, so that returning to the source, through which you are passing even now, you'll all the while feel *elsewhere*-headed, and blessed.

Goodbye, Jonas, and later to whomever you have pretended to have been. So long to your plights and gripes, your privileged indulgences, your poisoned irony, your violent innocence, your self-centred sense of shame. Please don't apologize; just go and disappear.

There are portals into the earth — choose the Jonas-shaped one. Descend the stairs to the underground club where writers and jazz musicians gather to trace their love back to the cobblestone alleys and neon-red streets of the previous century.

It's no surprise that covering cherub, Hart Crane is here, and Weldon Kees with his poised cigarette, and John Berryman inside his barbarian beard, and the unendurable fact of Sylvia Plath. And the Devil's Water is pouring in like music, as your breath disappears through golden tubes to re-emerge, resplendent!

Ah, so much for these other lives — the ones you were so blindly reaching out for. And your life of the mind? Your life of the senses? There still might be a clue in the zodiac of footprints around the skiff deserted at the water's edge...

(Or what remains is only poetry — for which we have yet to find any purpose or use.)

Notes

Epigraphs:

> Aristotle: *Poetics*, Part VIII
>
> William Wordsworth: *The Prelude*, 1805 ed., Book II
>
> Hart Crane: "Voyages," from *White Buildings*

11   Cf. Ezra Pound's "Canto I": "And then went down to the ship,/Set keel to breakers, forth on the godly sea."

      Cf. Odysseus and the Sirens in Homer's *Odyssey*, Book XII.

16   Cf. William Wordsworth's *Prelude*, 1805 ed., Book V: "Visionary power/Attends the motions of the viewless winds,/Embodied in the mystery of words."

19   The lines of poetry come from "The Spell of the Yukon," by Robert W. Service.

28   The Dwarf's song comes from "Insane in the Membrane," by Cypress Hill.

29   "Freedom's just another word for nothing left to lose" comes from "Me and Bobby McGee," by Kris Kristofferson and Fred Foster.

32   Cf. Homer's *Odyssey*, Book XVIII.

33   *Krapp's Last Tape* refers to the play by Samuel Beckett.

34   Cf. Fyodor Dostoevsky's *Crime and Punishment*.

36   Cf. Homer's *Odyssey*, Book XII.

49   "love thee better after death" comes from "How Do I Love Thee? (Sonnet 43)," by Elizabeth Barrett Browning.

50 Cf. William Blake's *The Marriage of Heaven and Hell*:

> The reason Milton wrote in fetters when he
> wrote of Angels & God, and at liberty when
> of Devils & Hell, is because he was a true Poet,
> and of the Devils party without knowing it.

"the breath, smiles, tears, of all your life" also comes from Barrett Browning's "How Do I Love Thee?"

52 Cf. Chris Hutchinson's "Dear Sidewalk," from *Other People's Lives*.

55 The Velvet Underground song referred to is "Heroin."

Cf. Elizabeth Smart's *By Grand Central Station I Sat Down and Wept*.

59 Cf. Jacques Derrida's writings on "*différance*."

Cf. Ernest Hemingway's *The Nick Adams Stories*.

61 *Iron John: A Book about Men* is by Robert Bly.

63 Cf. the Cyclops in Homer's *Odyssey*, Book XIV.

64 "Hell is other people" comes from Jean-Paul Sartre's play *No Exit*.

69 Cf. Federico Fellini's *La Dolce Vita*: "Hey, Paparazzo!"

77 *Les Enfants Terrible* is a novel by Jean Cocteau.

Cf. John B. Watson's *Psychological Care of Infant and Child*.

78-84 Cf. Chris Hutchinson's "The Idea of Forever," from *Unfamiliar Weather*.

88 The Led Zeppelin song referred to is "Dazed and Confused."

91 Cf. Italo Calvino's *The Baron in the Trees*.

94   Cf. Robert Lowell's "Skunk Hour."

97   Cf. William Shakespeare's *Richard III*.

99   Cf. Jules Verne's *Twenty Thousand Leagues under the Sea*.

100 Cf. William Shakespeare's *Hamlet*, Act II, Scene 2.

102 Cf. Ezra Pound's "Canto CXVI."

106 Cf. Martin Heidegger's *Being and Time*.

108 Cf. William Shakespeare's *Hamlet*, Act I, Scene 2.

116 "Danger, Will Robinson" comes from the 1960s American television series *Lost in Space*.

118 Cf. W.H. Auden's "In Memory of W. B. Yeats."

124 "Around the world, around the world" comes from the eponymous song by Daft Punk.

125 Cf. James Wright's "Lying in a Hammock at William Duffy's Farm in Pine Island, Minnesota."

127 Cf. Homer's *Odyssey*, Book XII.

128 Cf. Roald Dahl's *Charlie and the Chocolate Factory*: "the snozberries taste like snozberries!"

129 Cf. Frederick Goddard Tuckerman's sonnets.

131 "California Über Alles" is a song by the Dead Kennedys.

137 Cf. J.D. Salinger's *The Catcher in the Rye*.

138 "Can't beat the system. Go with the flow" comes from "I'm Riffin," by MC Duke.

139 "We Stay Up All Night" is by Buraka Sim Sistema.

143 Cf. Henry Wadsworth Longfellow's *Evangeline*, Part the First, III.

150   "trailing clouds of glory" comes from "Ode: Intimations of Immortality," by William Wordsworth.

151   "Up there is blue skies...he's looking at me" comes from "Blue Skies," by Dizzy Gillespie and Joe Carroll.

153   Cf. Sylvia Plath's "Cut."

157   Cf. Samuel Taylor Coleridge's "Kubla Khan."

159   "The world you desire...It is yours" comes from Ayn Rand's *Atlas Shrugged*.

170   "Da Ya Think I'm Sexy" is a song by Rod Stewart, Carmine Appice, and Duane Hitchings.

174   Cf. John Milton's "Lycidas," line 153.

176   "It seemed that this enthusiast...man of the world" comes from George Eliot's *Daniel Deronda*.

176-79 Cf. Samuel Taylor Coleridge's *The Rime of the Ancient Mariner*.

184   Cf. Don McKay's "The Great Blue Heron," from *Birding, or Desire*.

Acknowledgements

Bits and pieces of this book once appeared in disguise in my essay, "What Remains in the Kingdom of the Afterlife (Etc., and So On)," published in *Event Magazine*. Thanks to the editor, Elizabeth Bachinsky.

I'd like to acknowledge the London-based band Giant Burger (giantburger.bandcamp.com), whose music helped both to feed and assuage the various moods of my writing process.

Props to Alex Cieslik for his willingness and uncanny ability to translate words into visual mediums. Collaborations are a bitch, but I like to think that the dream of an illuminated manuscript is still in the offing.

For editorial support and encouragement, thanks to Matthew Brennan, Evie Christie, Katia Grubisic, Marguerite Pigeon, and Kevin Prufer. Special thanks to Matt Rader who was one of the first to suggest that the manuscript might find a life somewhere outside of my bottom desk drawer. This gratitude extends to everyone at Goose Lane and the whole icehouse poetry crew.

As always, I am supremely grateful to Meghan Martin, my most careful and demanding reader, my best editor, and my companion through all the storms.

Photo: Patrick Jandak

Chris Hutchinson was born in Montreal and grew up in Victoria, and has since lived in Vancouver, Dawson City, Kelowna, New York City, and Houston. His poems have appeared in numerous literary journals and anthologies in Canada and the US. He is also the author three collections of poetry: *A Brief History of the Short-lived*, *Other People's Lives*, and *Unfamiliar Weather*. *Jonas in Frames* is his fourth book of poetry and his first novel.